Durrington Detective Agency

By Derek McMillan

Edited by Angela McMillan

First published by CreateSpace in 2016

This edition 2019

All characters fictitious

Introduction

This is a collection of a dozen detective stories. It introduces the Durrington Detective Agency and the heroes, Craig McLairy, Micah McLairy and Barker who is sometimes called Hairy McLairy to differentiate him from bald Craig. There are a host of other characters who fulfil the role of murderer, murderee or that classic in detective fiction the red herring.

We were inspired by Jeanne M Dams whose detective stories are referred to as 'cozy'. All that means is that there is no graphic sex or violence. The same term could apply to most of Agatha Christie's books.

I do hope this book does not make Durrington into an equivalent of Oxford, Midsomer or anything in the orbit of Miss Marple – a place where you won't live long.

Many of the locations are real. The John Selden for example is a first-rate pub and within walking distance of our home which is convenient. All the references to people are fictitious.

At the sign of the John Selden

We ate at the John Selden because we could both dine quite well on one course with two sets of cutlery. Micah, my partner in crime-fighting, had chosen the beer-battered cod which was quite enough fish for a small family.

The landlady was pacifying Barker with dog treats on a lavish scale. Micah insisted on calling him Hairy McLairy and calling me Baldy McLairy. She is funny like that.

We were enjoying the coffee when she put on her business face and spoke quietly to me.

"Craig, what do you think about our case?"

It was a fiction to call it a case since we were not being paid for it. A friend of ours, George Farnsworth, had been found dead in his home. He had had a history of heart trouble which led Doctor Winter to sign it off as 'natural causes'. Micah and I thought differently.

"You reject the idea of a random burglar?"

"Well even an incompetent windbag like Winter would have noticed if the house had been ransacked."

"Exactly." Micah crossed "burglar" out on her notepad. She continued, "Did George have any enemies?"

Then she answered her own question. "None that we know of."

She put a question mark next to "enemies".

"I was chatting to Mary." Micah looked puzzled so I expanded, "Mary Doats, the Farnsworth's cook. It seems that Gerald had an almighty row with George a month or so back. George had had the cheek to suggest the little layabout should get a job and words like 'sponger' and 'parasite' were used."

"Proper little earwigger, your friend Mary."

"Well earwiggers can be very useful to us and Mary is not my friend. I am just generally well-disposed towards people."

Micah wrote 'Gerald' in her notebook and said, "I had better add Kitty and Hermione as well to be fair. Neither of them have jobs. I know Kitty volunteers for the Sally Army and Hermione has her Cat Protection League but neither of them has a paying job."

"So they all ganged up on poor old George?"

"'Poor old' my Aunt Fanny, he left over a million."

"And don't forget the value of the house if those three sloths can ever organise themselves to sell it."

When Micah had written, Gerald, Kitty and Hermione in her notebook she looked at it darkly for a moment and then suggested, "How about another Cabernet Sauvignon while we think about this?"

I agreed. Merlot is inoffensive, Shiraz has something more about it but I have never met a Cabernet Sauvignon I didn't like.

After a while, Micah had an idea. "Gerald is trying to find a buyer for George's old computer."

"Surely he will delete everything on it before he sells it."

"And would you trust Gerald to wipe a hard drive? Or to run a booze-up in a brewery come to that."

"And you think you can undelete anything he has deleted."

"I would bet my pension on it," said Micah decisively.

"And it would be a chance to talk to Gerald, possibly his sisters too."

George's house was within walking distance of the John Selden. I rang George's number and eventually Gerald summoned up the energy to reply.

"Are you still looking for a buyer for George's old computer?"

"Well it seems to be a bit of a drug on the market. I have to warn you that it is very old."

"Why don't we come round and have a look at it?"

"Well," (why did Gerald begin every sentence with 'well'?) "I suppose so but you might be wasting your time. Well, don't say I didn't warn you."

When we arrived the house did look as if it had been ransacked by a careless burglar but we guessed this was just the result of the three younger Farnsworths taking a relaxed attitude to tidying up.

"Oh Gerald, it must have been such a shock for you, finding old George's body like that." Micah was putting on her mother hen act. It was a good act.

"Well it was a while before we found the body. Pater always locked the bathroom door when he was having a bath so we had to decide something was wrong and then break down the door."

"It was you who found the body?"

"Well yes, why do you ask?"

"Where is this computer then?" Micah changed the subject.

While Micah was looking at the computer I decided I needed to answer a call of nature. Gerald directed me to the bathroom although I already knew where it was from previous visits.

I was glad to see George had finally removed the old one-bar electric fire from the wall above the bath. His friends had been telling him it was a hazard for years but George was nothing if not stuck in his ways. And then of course it struck me, the electric fire wouldn't bother George where he'd gone.

I flushed the loo and ran the taps for appearances' sake and rejoined Micah in the living room. The smell from the kitchen told me Mary was cooking up one of her wonderful meals and I mentioned as much to Gerald.

"Oh Mary," he shouted into the kitchen, lacking the energy or the manners to go in person to talk to a servant, "Well I actually won't be in for dinner tonight. Off out with friends."

We arranged to collect the computer, an old desktop model, the following day.

As luck would have it, Hermione was there so we didn't have to make a special trip to the Cat Protection League to talk to her.

"The computer? What computer?"

"Your father's computer. Gerald sold it to us for twenty pounds."

"Well he had no right to do so! That is Gerald all over. Did you get a receipt?"

"No but we gave him the money."

"How do I know?"

"Hermione, I have known you since you were this high," I demonstrated with my palm.

"Yes I know, Craig and I know I'm being silly but you have to be so careful to make sure people aren't cheating you." She stopped for a moment and then went on, "I didn't mean you, of course not."

"Who did you mean?" asked Micah.

"I don't like to say."

Hermione didn't like to say but that only meant she wanted us to coax the information out of her. Micah was an ace coaxer and Hermione eventually came out with the following:

"It's Gerald. You knew didn't you? Father and Gerald had one big row and a hundred little ones about money. Now he is rushing to turn everything into cash. I am sure he would sell me into white slavery if he could get away with it. Well perhaps not but he is a mercenary little...er mercenary."

We got on to the subject of George's death and she complained that Gerald was being "all mysterious" about it. He hadn't let either of his sisters into the bathroom for ages.

"That might have been just, you know, to give him time to cover old George up."

"Yes. Except that now I think about it he hadn't covered him up. He was moving stuff around in the bathroom. Only father and Gerald ever used it. Kitty and I prefer the shower room."

"I think we should be fair and have a word with Kitty."

We caught up with Kitty at the Salvation Army shop.

"Oh Craig, Micah. It is so nice to see a friendly face. I come here to get away from Hermione and Gerald rowing. It is a pity you don't come round any more. Things were so much better then. When daddy was alive, Gerald was a beast but now he's become a super-beast. The things he calls Hermione. And the things she calls him! I didn't know they taught that sort of language at Roedean.

"I say, are you y'know investigating this? I know you always fancied yourself as a tec, a private tec of course."

"We couldn't possibly say."

Her eyes widened, "You ARE! Well I can tell you who I suspect. Mary. She could have poisoned him."

"Did she have a motive?"

"None that we know of but servants are always underpaid aren't they?"

"Not that many end up murdering the people who underpay them and Doctor Winter would have noticed if his patient had been poisoned surely. There might have been a scent of bitter almonds or traces of cyanide in the bloodstream, that kind of thing."

"Don't patronise me!" Kitty shouted and almost threw us out of the shop.

"That girl has a temper on her." Micah observed mildly.

"She certainly has."

"Mmm this wasn't a crime of anger or passion though. This was a cold-blooded murder."

"Well let's see what that computer has to tell us."

The computer spoke volumes. There were emails. A lady called Marion Locke featured a lot in them. Marion was the Chief Executive of Benevolent Chemicals Ltd but as her correspondence with George progressed she became less and less benevolent.

George accused her point blank of experimenting on animals. She firstly denied all knowledge. Then George produced evidence. She wanted to know where the evidence came from. Then she abruptly changed tack and started defending testing on animals and accusing George (George with his lifelong pacifism and dicky ticker!) of being a terrorist.

The final email, chillingly just one week before George's death, was as follows. "I have wasted too much of my valuable time on this correspondence. You will not repeat any of your allegations. If you do so, you will be silenced."

We sent her an email asking if her firm engaged in animal testing.

She sent a reply the same day.

"Benevolent Chemicals Ltd only makes a minimal use of animal testing and we follow government guidelines. We do not wish to receive any more correspondence from animal rights activists and if we do we will take steps to ensure that they cease."

Micah replied, "Was one of the animals you experimented on the late George Farnsworth?"

There was a delay before Marion Locke replied to this, so Micah sent in a supplementary question.

"Would you care to elaborate on your use of the phrase "you will be silenced." in your correspondence with the late George Farnsworth? We would appreciate a face-to-face interview to clarify this matter. We are reluctant at this stage to involve the police."

That did get a reply. It came from one Thomas Thorson, PA to Marion Locke. After a preamble about how terribly busy Ms Locke was, he then gave us an appointment for the following day.

I put the kettle on and we arranged our day over a couple of flat whites. I rang the dog walker to see if she was available to look after Barker. I was fairly sure that Ms Locke would not spontaneously experiment on any dog that came near her but I was not taking any chances. Micah had no time for animal rights activists but the thought of letting Barker anywhere near "that woman" made her blood boil.

We googled the offices of Benevolent Chemicals Ltd and found a good restaurant nearby where we could lunch before meeting La Locke.

The portions were not of the same magnitude as those at the John Seldon but they were quite adequate. I had lamb because there was no way Micah would eat it at home so I only ate it when we were dining out. As a gesture to animal welfare, Micah consented to the vegetarian option which was a pizza. I tried some of it. It was excellent. We settled for one glass of Cabernet Sauvignon each because we needed to keep a clear head between us. The quality of the wine more than made up for the quantity.

We were not prepared for Ms Locke however. She really did look the part of a benevolent chemist and she was in a wheelchair.

Seeing my look, she felt she had to say, "You are right in thinking that a cure for polio only came about by animal experiments. Slightly too late for me, as you can see."

"So how did you feel about George attacking your experiments on animals?"

"How do you think? Now I really am a very busy executive and I do not need to rehearse all the pros and cons with you. Did you have a specific question?"

Before I could speak, Micah jumped in with, "So why didn't you tell George what you just told us?"

"It was none of his business." she said sharply. Then she continued in a more mellow vein, "I am shy. That may seem ridiculous but it's true. And I am just a little sick of people comparing me with Eisenhower. My lawyers advised me that I could silence Mr Farnsworth..."

"Doctor Farnsworth," I corrected.

"I could silence him. And you will know that he sent me no more emails after I told him as much."

"He was dead." I said neutrally.

"Nothing to do with me or Benevolent Chemicals. I intended to silence him by legal means. Murder would have been unnecessary although I understand his death was attributed to natural causes. Now you have taken up enough of my time. You may leave."

We left.

"So do we put Marion Locke on our list now?"

"I don't think he was killed by a person in a wheelchair. The bathroom is on the first floor."

"So Marion Locke's minions then?"

I agreed and Micah put "minion?" on her growing list of suspects.

We were surprised to see Kitty waiting on our doorstep when we got home.

"I just had to see you, I just had to. I mean after I was so rude to you and all that, I had to apologise and all that."

I did wonder what "all that" was but I kept my peace.

"I told you that I knew Mary Doats was the murderer and you rather pooh-poohed the idea. Well now I have proof. What do you think about this?"

And she brought a packet of garden weedkiller from her shopping basket.

"Aren't you going to ask me where I found this?"

"Where did you find it?" asked Micah, who has more patience than I have.

"In the cupboard under the sink in the kitchen of the innocent Mary Doats!" she crowed.

There are advantages in having a daughter in the medical profession. Micah always reminds me of this when I am crotchety about the fees we had to pay for Dorothy's extended education. We invited her round for a meal although with her salary and our pensions she should be feeding us – another of those things Micah thinks I am crotchety about.

We had a very special arrabiata without garlic or chillies but plenty of bacon. Dorothy to her credit had brought a very fine bottle of Rioja. She also made a fuss over Barker which I like to see,

Eventually as an aside I mentioned the weedkiller question.

"Well you could never poison anybody with that," Dorothy was quite certain, "It is safe for pets and wild animals too. They don't make weedkillers that kill humans these days – not without a warning in very large letters for people with very small brains.

Micah started singing "It's beginning to look a lot like Gerald," in a parody of a Christmas song.

"We will confront him tomorrow." I said.

"What is all this about, dad?"

"Well you've forced me to tell you all about it, remember that when you get bored." I told her the whole story with generally useful interruptions from Micah.

"Just watch yourself, yourselves really. You are not as young as you were and if this Gerald is a murderer, you could just be his next victim."

"I don't know, I'm pretty handy with the old judo, you know."

Dorothy and Micah laughed at that and I thought it wise to join in.

As we were turning in for the night, Micah's final remark of the evening was, "We need a cunning plan. I know in *Murder She Wrote,* the villains always confess. In real life I think we'd have to inject Gerald with the truth drug to get anything out of him. And the truth drug is a myth."

My dreams were filled with cunning plans to get the truth out of Gerald but most of them were impractical and involved the use of the rack – an ancient method of proven efficacy in extracting confessions from innocent and guilty alike. Then I came back to the one thing I knew about Gerald. Gerald was pathologically lazy. If he were the murderer then he would have been lazy in disposing of the murder weapon and in covering his tracks.

We visited George's house once again. The three layabouts were laying about elsewhere. While I engaged Mary Doats in conversation, Micah had to answer a call of nature. She called via Gerald's room, the basement and the shed. She returned to the kitchen and gave me a thumbs up.

"When is Gerald due back?"

"I think all three of them will be back for dinner. It's not the same since Dr Farnsworth went on to a better place, it really isn't."

"Can you manage a couple of extra for dinner?"

"Of course. Have you been invited?"

It was the work of a minute to arrange an invitation from Kitty. I may have hinted that I was about to perform a citizen's arrest on Mary Doats.

The family assembled for dinner and they greeted us civilly enough. I had spent the intervening period looking at Micah's phone and visiting the shed. I came back with a carrier bag.

Mary was right. It was not the same as when George was alive. It was more like feeding time at the zoo. Gerald's table manners, his inability to close his mouth while eating and his apparent lack of knowledge of knives and fork, should have been enough to have him locked up without the little business of murder.

When the menagerie had finished feeding, I said, "I have a picture to show you." I passed round Micah's phone.

The first picture showed the fuse box. George had never had it modernised and it showed a shiny new fuse wire where someone had had to fix a fuse quite recently.

"Well that's bloody boring." Gerald said. His siblings seemed to agree.

"How about this."

It was a photo of Gerald's bedroom wall, the wall which was next to the bathroom. There was a crack in the plaster and the evidence that it had been hit with a blunt instrument. Gerald was silent.

I explained matter-of-factly, "If somebody, Gerald, had hit that wall after loosening the screws holding up the electric fire over the bath, the fire would have fallen into the water."

"Ah but the electric fire had been removed months ago." Gerald said cunningly.

I put the clearly fused electric fire on the table.

"No, Gerald it was removed on the night Dr Farnsworth died. Removed by you. But you are such a lazy slob you only removed it as far as the shed."

"Well you are wrong there Mr Smarty-pants. I put it under the bed first before moving it to the...."

Did I mention that in addition to being lazy and ill-mannered, Gerald wasn't particularly bright? So we didn't need the truth drug after all.

"Mary I believe you have been entertaining DI Chambers in the kitchen?"

"Well I don't know about entertaining but she has been writing down everything Master Gerald said."

After Gerald was led away in handcuffs and DI Chambers took temporary charge of Micah's phone, she turned to me.

"Well what shall we do now?"

"Well it isn't closing time at the John Selden yet."

High Flyer

The girl at the table was what my old mother would call a suicide blonde – dyed by her own hand. It was not until she turned round and I saw her prodigious nose in profile that I realised it was my sister. The last time I saw her, her hair was jet black or red or perhaps brunette. It was difficult to keep track. Mama had warned her that one day it would all fall out and she would be left with nothing but multi-coloured dandruff.

"Craig!" she cried with fake enthusiasm.

"Clarissa!" I could match her fake for fake.

"It's been such a long time..."

"How's your leg?"

"What have you been doing with yourself?"

"Still in the same old..."

The questions tumbled over each other and I could tell she was not listening to the answers.

She was dining alone and she invited me to join her, after I had sat down. I ordered the filet mignon and suggested she do likewise.

"It's particularly good here."

"Ah but I have become a vegan, if you know what one of those is."

"An inhabitant of Vega?" I hazarded.

"You are bloody childish, Craig."

"How long have you been a vegan?"

"About a week."

"The longest week of your life?"

Clarissa had the good manners to laugh at that anyway.

"You know I am glad I bumped into you, Craig. Something very strange has happened. Very strange indeed."

Now she had my interest and I listened carefully to the tale she unfolded.

"You know Mr Mitchell. Actually you don't know him. You wouldn't move in the same circles. Charlie Mitchell is quite a high flier."

"Air force?"

"Shut up and listen, Craig."

I shut up. I listened.

"Charlie works for Allied Consolidated and he is tipped to be the next CEO. That's 'Chief Executive Officer' to you. Well, he got into a bit of trouble. I'll have a glass of the Champers if it's Moet (this last remark was addressed to a waitress. For the record I chose the Shiraz.) Now where was I? Oh yes. Charlie got into a bit of a fix over a car. It wasn't his fault. Well he was in the driving seat. He reversed over a blind man. Well he was in his blind spot you see. We all laughed about that. And anyway what are blind people doing walking the streets I'd like to know?"

"I was very sorry his dog had to be put down. Those seeing-eye dogs are so clever and it takes ages to train them."

"What happened to the blind man?"

"Oh he died I think. I'm not sure. Do let me get on, Craig. The thing is, Charlie has disappeared. His bed wasn't slept in. His servant found the master had vanished without taking any of his clothes which was very strange. So I am sure you have nothing important on, Craig and I know you've always wanted to be a private dick. We laughed about that too. So find him."

"I'm afraid I only work for money."

"How boringly mercenary of you. Well Charlie has 'loadsa money' as they say so I am sure he will be able to pay you. If and when you find him."

"Alive." I said

"What was that? Now don't be morbid, Craig. I am sure this is a very simple case or I wouldn't give it to you. You are pretty useless after all."

I wearily took out a notebook. The latest notes were a shopping list. I didn't get much work but I had a pension.

"What is the name of the servant?"

"Jeeves? I can't remember the names of menials. You will find him at Charlie's flat."

She gave me the address and a key which she just happened to have.

My nasty suspicious mind made me wonder if she knew more about the disappearance of Charlie 'loadsamoney' Mitchell than she was letting on.

"Jeeves", whose name turned out to be Lawrence Aloysius Wilkins, was very helpful.

"Mr Mitchell was wearing the clothes he put on that morning, an Armani suit (one of the solid slim-fit in blue, purchased the previous week. They are rather nice.) His shirt was a lighter shade of blue which matched his eyes. He also wore a new pair of Italian shoes, leather lace-ups and rather old-fashioned if I may say so."

"How would he get about?"

"He will have to use public transport. That inconsiderate blind man made a mess of his car and it is still in the garage. I have checked. They have completed work on it and are asking for money. Tradesmen can be so mercenary, don't you find?"

"What are you doing for money? Mr Mitchell cannot pay your wages."

"They are paid automatically, sir, by his bank. I wouldn't leave something like that to chance. Mr Mitchell, although one shouldn't speak ill of the dead ..I mean missing... would tend to forget things like that. He had so many important things to think about, you know."

I said goodbye to Lawrence and made a phone call. One of my old Eton chums was a Chief Ticket Inspector or Lord High Panjandrum or whatnot with the rozzers. I tapped him for some rather specific information about our Lawrence. At first he said he hadn't got it but I reminded him of some of the larks we used to get up to as lads and he suddenly remembered he had an analysis of CCTV evidence which might be of some use to me. Who says the old school tie doesn't cut the mustard?

Lawrence had apparently visited a charity shop. This was out of character. He didn't seem the charitable type

...

"What can I do for you, love?"

"Well I have a question. Did a man come into this shop on Tuesday? Dapper young chap with a mole on his neck. Not your usual sort of customer, I imagine."

"Well it wasn't me, it was Else but she remembered your friend. He was very smartly dressed but he bought the sort of clothes Else thought he wouldn't be seen dead in."

She gave me a description of the clothes and 'Else', whoever she was, had the right of it. Lawrence wouldn't be seen dead in those clothes. A fitting turn of phrase as it happened.

I took to going round to cheer up Lawrence and he seemed glad of the company. Poor Lawrence had developed a taste for the good life which he could not possibly afford. I noted that the supply of single malt whisky had somehow evaporated. On my next meeting, I brought Lawrence a little present in the form of Jura Superstition and we shared it.

"In vino veritas" refers to the discovery by the ancient Romans that after drinking of the grape a fellow will spill the beans if you will pardon the omnivorous metaphor.

Our Lawrence was no exception. Some time between deciding I was his best mate in the world and offering to fight any man in the house (there were just the two of us), he came clean.

"Your sister, Carlissa, Crissa. She is a damned fine girl. Yes a damn fine girl. Too good for that scoundrel Charlie Mitchell anyway. I told her as much."

"What was your relationship with Clarissa?"

He repeated what a damned fine girl she was and eventually described their relationship as "close".

"What made Charlie Mitchell a 'scoundrel' though?"

"Well I'll tell you. I'll tell you. Well I'll tell you!"

"What will you tell me."

"Crissa thought she was pregnant and that scoundrel got her to take some foul pills which made her very ill but didn't cause an abortion because you see. You see?"

"See what?"

"Well she wasn't ruddy pregnant was she?"

Lawrence gave me a cunning look, "I tell you what though. I got my own back on that scoundrel. I dissolved some of those foul pills in his soup. That told him!"

"And what happened to him?"

"Well thas for me to know and you to..you to..." and he fell asleep. When he awoke he was belligerent and not answering any questions.

My next port of call was the sea-front at Worthing. My chum in the rozzers had let me know that Lawrence's number-plate had been recorded in Worthing around the time Charlie disappeared.

There are little shelters along the sea front which are built in a pseudo-chinese style. They are known locally as 'tramps' hotels'. The local paper had a picture of a mystery tramp whose body had been discovered in one of them. One look at the picture told me all I wanted to know.

I reported the identity of the victim and the murderer to the local police and made an appointment for lunch with Clarissa at the John Selden.

The food was as excellent as ever, I had the roast pork and Clarissa had the scampi and we shared a very fine bottle of French plonk. Clarissa was off her food though and less that pleased with me for getting her boyfriend arrested. She would never have made the connection between a 'high flier' like Charlie and a dead tramp. It was of course the charity shop which made the connection. Lawrence had bought clothes to dress Charlie as a tramp before depositing the body.

In the end Clarissa was philosophical about it. "Well rather Lawrence than me!" she said as she downed the last of the Chateau de Plonk.

It was a funny case

"He makes more on cards than he does on horses. You see he can't deal the horses."

Trevor didn't mind that the joke was as old as he was. The drinkers in The John Selden were an easy-going crowd and they laughed anyway.

"Who is Trev talking about?" Micah asked.

"Councillor Alberto Friedrich," I said, "He doesn't bet on horses nor on cards but Trev is right in one thing. Friedrich is as bent as a corkscrew as the saying goes."

"How do you know?"

"He was a clerical assistant with expensive tastes. Now he has a seafront apartment worth two million which he owns outright and a roller."

Micah frowned.

"A Rolls Royce," I said.

"Yes," she said patiently, "I know that but your evidence, Mr McLairy, is purely circumstantial."

"I suppose it is, Mrs McLairy, but that is how they caught Al Capone. His lifestyle had a plain disparity with his declared income."

"Al Capone?" She laughed, "In Worthing?"

Barker looked up from his doggie snacks as if to suggest he thought this was a ludicrous idea too.

We talked about other things and forgot about Friedrich until I bought that week's *Worthing Herald.*

The newspaper normally headlines charity walks, planning disputes and flower shows. This week it ran with "Councillor fatally stabbed through the mouth."

With a momentary uncharitable thought about how appropriate an end that was for a windbag, I read on.

"The body of Councillor Alberto Friedrich was found early on Saturday morning in his luxury seafront apartment with a knife wound to the mouth and throat. The body was found by his maid, Tilly McGregor, who commented, 'He was a nice kind man without an enemy in the world except UKIP and the Russians of course. I want to know how I am going to get all the blood out for this nice Persian carpet. He brought it back special from his fact-finding visit to the middle east.'

"Friedrich was a well-liked and respected local councillor and will be sadly missed."

"Stabbed through the mouth. It suggests someone wanted Alberto Friedrich silenced," Micah suggested.

"It seems to have worked."

"That is not helpful, Craig. The police will be all over this one. Let's see how they are getting on."

Micah used her dark arts on the laptop to hack into the police computers. These days the police don't have to rely on notebooks. All the evidence is collated on a system only they can access. (Or so they think.)

One DCI used a laptop and by accessing this, Micah could access all the data on the killing.

"Bent as a corkscrew," Micah said. "Your evidence was merely circumstantial but the police have access to his accounts, open and secret and they have turned up quite a lot of nefarious jiggery-pokery.

"Friedrich fiddled his expenses. I know all politicians do that but this was on a quite spectacular scale. A lot of interest focuses on his fact-finding mission to the middle east. Why a seaside town like Worthing has any need of fact-finding tours of the middle east nobody knows but Friedrich was careful to include other worthies in his tours and he treated them lavishly with money from a hitherto mysterious source."

"But it is mysterious no longer?" I suggested.

"Well the way the money was filtered through fake companies and false bank accounts took some investigation. Now the police have tracked down the source of the money." Micah paused.

"Well don't keep me in suspense."

"The source was Alberto Friedrich himself. You know all that work he did for charity? Well the police calculate the charities in question received about 50% of the dosh."

"But surely the charities would know they were being diddled."

"He was always sure to support several charities at once so their accounting systems wouldn't show this up. The Battered Bunnies thought the money had gone to Deaf Dogs and vice versa."

"Well wouldn't they..."

"They don't talk to each other."

"That's ridiculous."

"Tell them that. I already know.

"Friedrich wasn't married but he had a live-in girlfriend, Cynthia Tress who was conveniently absent visiting a sick aunt in Birmingham. The police checked out the alibi and they found it was valid. The aunt was something of a hypochondriac and she was always 'ill' but this time she was actually in hospital."

"There is nothing quite so suspicious as a water-tight alibi." I said.

"That's true," Micah agreed.

"There was no evidence, DNA or fingerprints, on the knife. It was an ordinary kitchen knife and probably belonged to Friedrich. It is assumed that Friedrich had a meal with someone on the night in question. I can give you a list of his stomach contents if you like but there is nothing outré about them. The dishwasher had been run so there was no evidence to indicate who that 'someone' might have been.

"They have drawn up a list of Friedrich's known associates so we might as well start from there. It seems likely he knew his attacker."

Barker had been whining for a walk so we agreed I would take him for one and then we settled down to think about suspects.

"Remember the symbolism of stabbing Friedrich through the mouth. Somebody wanted him silenced. We have his fellow councillors and I have circled the ones who went on his fact-finding jaunts. Unfortunately, they are all minuted as attending a council committee meeting that evening so they alibi each other."

"Didn't they think it odd that Friedrich didn't attend?"

"Friedrich was not on the committee in question so he wouldn't have attended anyway. And before you ask they have ruled out the possibility that he accidentally stabbed himself through the mouth. He is unlikely to have run the dishwasher after his death."

"Who arranged the middle east jolly?"

"Apart from Friedrich himself there was a Mr Aziz. He has no known terrorist affiliations. I noticed they only checked Mr Aziz for those, nobody else. He is a well-heeled and well-respected events organiser. He claimed not to know the mysterious source of Friedrich's cash. He didn't enquire too closely of course. Neither did any of the councillors or Cynthia Tress for that matter."

"Is she the daughter of ..."

"Councillor Robert Tress. Yes. And he was one of the group who went to the middle east at Friedrich's expense. So did his daughter. They both have good alibis you remember."

Our first port of call was Aziz Events' Management.

"My name is Francis Thompson of Thompson's Foods. I am interested in arranging a visit for like-minded businessmen to the middle east. Councillor Friedrich recommended your services to us and I wonder if..."

"I know exactly who you are, Mr McLairy of 'McLairy and McLairy. Private Investigations undertaken, full discretion assured' so you can desist from beating about the mulberry bush if you will be so kind.

"I imagine you are investigating the murder of my friend, Alberto Friedrich Junior. I resent your disingenuous approach, Mr McLairy. I expect you had your reasons. If you had approached me openly I would have been equally open with you."

"I will only say that I arranged a fact-finding mission to the middle east for councillors. I was unaware of the financing arrangements. You will appreciate that 'discretion assured' ought also to be on my business cards. So long as I was reimbursed the matter was no concern of mine."

"Now good day, Mr McLairy, I trust there will be no more visits from you. I would not like to call the police and have you removed from the premises."

Micah, Barker and I met up at the dog-friendly John Selden for lunch and dog biscuits. The lunch was excellent. As usual we shared the meal. It was a massive roast pork dinner with four vegetables, and there was plenty for both of us. I explained how Aziz had blown my cover without any difficulty and I played back to Micah the recording I had made on my mobile phone.

Micah said one word.

"Junior?"

"That means," my thoughts unfolded more slowly than Micah's most of the time, "that there must be an Alberto Friedrich Senior."

"There is," Micah was fiddling with her phone, "and his address is just round the corner in Durrington. I could go and talk to him on behalf of *Worthing Today*, take some photos, show an interest in his son etc. And hopefully not blow my cover like an amateur."

I was about to protest about this but I thought better of it...

"Ungrateful little swine." was Mr Friedrich Senior's comment on his late son.

"I was going to say that I am very sorry for your loss."

"Well of course. I would not wish to speak ill of the dead. It is just that when he was alive he was an ungrateful little swine. That's all."

"Can you tell us anything about his childhood?"

"Yes he was an ungrateful little swine then. He was the death of his poor mother. And do you know. Do you know, he wasn't just ungrateful to me, oh no. He used to rail in English – the only language he ever knew – against the English. And then look at the posh house, posh bird and posh car he ended up with. I ask you. England did well enough for him. Oh yes."

"And do you think he gave a brass farthing, whatever one of those is, to his old dad? What do you think? What do you think?"

There is a pause in the recording. Micah remained wisely silent. We ask the questions.

"No nothing!"

(Micah records that at this point Friedrich senior leant dangerously close to her and the odour of lager was overpowering)

"Now about these photos. You will say what a good boy he was and how his old dad is heartbroken won't you. Oh just make something up. It's what you journalists do isn't it, darling?"

Micah dutifully took the photos and came home to where a new addition to the kitchen, a washing machine, was arriving. This event was ably supervised by Barker and myself. When it had been installed, or 'plumbed in' I believe they call it, I noticed there was something inside it. Curious I opened the door and I found a small doll, a poppet, with a suitably small knife thrust into its mouth and protruding out the back. I rescued it from Barker before he destroyed the evidence.

"It is a voodoo doll." I suggested.

"No. Voodoo does not make use of dolls, it is a sign of European witchcraft." Micah corrected.

"So we are up against witches?"

"Hardly. This is a warning to us. As straightforward as the warning to Councillor Friedrich but fortunately less fatal. We should take this to the police as soon as possible."

To say that the constabulary were overwhelmed by the sight of me turning up at the desk at the local station with a shoebox containing the offending poppet would be an exaggeration. They dismissed me as a crank and sent me off to the local coven for advice.

Micah had more luck with Friedrich's solicitors, Badger and Sons. Naturally she didn't go to their office. She penetrated the laughable security on their computer system. Indeed she left a note suggesting ways they could improve their security. First, however, she found out who the beneficiary of Friedrich's will was.

It turned out that it was a Society for Cats with Hearing Difficulties. The Society got a cool six million from the estate and of course they benefited from the usual tax advantages which charities receive. The Board of Trustees of the Charity consisted of Cynthia Tress and three other individuals who turned out to be fictitious. The Chief Executive, on a salary of £150,000 (which was actually modest for a charity), was also Cynthia Tress.

Once again the one with the perfect alibi turned out to be the main beneficiary of the crime she could not possibly have committed.

Micah made a list of suspects. She then crossed off everyone with a good alibi. There was nobody on the list when she had completed this operation. Then she wrote down Alberto Friedrich Senior. After a while she added a question mark. Then she added Mr Aziz with another question mark. She dismissed as frivolous my suggestion that a cabal of deaf cats might have done him in.

"We need to talk to Cynthia Tress." I suggested.

"I need to talk to Cynthia Tress." Micah suggested.

I took Barker down to the seaside, which he always enjoys. By the time I got back, Micah was in the kitchen looking crestfallen. Her interview with Cynthia Tress was on her phone.

"I don't have to talk to you. My lawyer tells me I don't have to talk to you. You're with the press, aren't you? Why not just admit it? You're with the Worthing something-or-other aren't you? Can't you see I'm terribly upset about poor Alberto, he was just such an adorable man. What with that and my sister being ill..."

"Your aunt being ill?"

"Yes I meant my aunt. She was like a sister to me. You won't catch me out with any of your fancy questions so I will just say 'Good day' to you. No offence but you really should go. Now."

When she had played this to me, I pointed out the two things I had noticed and she cheered up considerably.

"So," she said, "we now know from Cynthia's remarks who committed the murder but the trick will be to prove it. We only have a guess but I do not doubt the guess."

"Neither do I."

In the TV shows someone who commits one murder is then constrained to commit another and it is at that point that Barnaby or Miss Marple can trap them. In real life the murderer might be quite happy with the outcome and no further crimes would be necessary.

"Unless of course..." Micah just kept the idea hanging. We both knew that a Private Investigator or a reporter who knew the identity of the murderer might end up dead.

"So if we play our cards close to our chest we won't risk a sticky end?" was her eventual conclusion.

"That is a rubbish metaphor but yes, I agree. We will just have to bide our time."

"Should I insert the name of the murderer into the police files?"

"Well our evidence is a bit nebulous. I think we can afford to wait. Perhaps you should leave an email to be sent to the police in case you do get murdered."

"Or you."

"Or me."

So we watched and we waited, waited and watched. We thought it unlikely that the murderer would be able to keep away from Cynthia for long. In the event he was more patient than we had given him credit for.

The police had not closed the file – it was a murder after all – but after six months the investigation had wound down. The press continued to pursue the issue but even they tired eventually. We were made of sterner stuff. There is also the detail that we didn't have any actual cases to pursue at the time.

In the end we were rewarded. Micah and I both approached the seafront flat with some trepidation. We were taking a gamble.

After a suitable delay, Cynthia opened the door. She was wearing a red dressing gown with CT monogrammed on the shoulder.

"We think we can tell you the identity of the murderer of your adorable Alberto."

"What?"

"We knew you would be pleased." She looked about as happy as a sandboy with dermatitis.

"You see it was your confusion of generations which gave you away. You think of your aunt as a sister? And your lover's father as a lover?

"And then there was your certainty that Micah worked for the Worthing Something-or-other. Only Alberto Friedrich senior had that piece of misleading information. Alberto, you may as well come out now."

A rather shamefaced Alberto Senior emerged from the bedroom wearing a similar dressing gown with AF on the shoulder.

"What gave you away," Micah took up the story, "was an observant van driver. You were seen putting an object into our new washing machine. That incriminating object is now in the hands of the police."

That wasn't strictly true but it was enough. Cynthia reacted like a bad-tempered whirlwind.

"You bloody idiot. You couldn't leave well enough alone could you?"

"Well," he adopted an unattractive whining tone, "Aziz warned me that McLairy was looking into things so I thought..."

"You thought! You thought! You never bloody think. I had to organise the alibi and everything. All you had to do was stab the ungrateful little swine but you had to do it through the mouth. What was all that about?"

Micah had already called the police and they arrived on cue. She handed over the recording in which the suspects incriminated each other. The police had the good grace to ask for the poppet with the knife through the mouth as evidence. That was a pity really as I had grown quite fond of the little chap although he did have a sharp tongue.

Malapert

We were sitting over an excellent meal in the Vintner's Parrot. Micah was having the baked potato with chilli con carne and I was having the best Whitby bay scampi in Sussex. We had a bottle of Casillero del Diablo Cabernet Sauvignon. The legend has it that the original owner of the cellars where the famous Cabernet Sauvignon was stored told everyone the devil lived there to discourage burglars. Perhaps a night watchman would have been a good idea.

While we ate, Barker was having himself groomed by his Furry Godmother. The Parrot does not encourage dogs or dog owners.

When we were sufficiently full to consider business, Micah told me about that rare entity, a case. To say we had few cases would be an understatement. The nephew of a Miss Malapert had come to us because he was unsatisfied with the doctor's verdict on her death.

"Dr Winter, who gives incompetent windbags a bad name, had diagnosed a cardiac arrest. The nephew, young Matt Malapert, said that everybody who is dead has a cardiac arrest and he refused to believe his tough old aunt had a dicky ticker."

Micah revealed that she had been using her dark arts to hack into Edie Malapert's medical records.

"And I found her repeat prescription very revealing. I looked for beta blockers. ACE inhibitors or any of the usual paraphernalia which accompanies heart trouble. They are significant for their absence."

"Was she on Statins?" I asked, to show I knew at least one medicine.

"Yes but then so is everybody over 50 so it is not conclusive. The only other thing on her medical record of interest was a referral for a hearing test. She had been referred to Specsavers."

"And what was the result?"

Micah looked crestfallen. "I can only say that Specsavers have better data encryption than the doctor. I can hack it if I have a clear day. I will let you know as soon as I have the information.

"Miss Edie Malapert lived alone in a decaying terrace of old houses. To her left was a household of noisy students and the house to the right was boarded up."

"Let's get over there to see what we can find out. I will talk to the students first."

"**We** will talk to the students first." Micah corrected.

She was right of course, her skills at interrogation equalled my own. A freshly groomed Barker would come too.

As is often the case, Barker was the ice-breaker. The door was answered by a young man in tattered jeans and his early twenties with a surly expression on his face. This changed to a beam when he greeted Barker with the 'Hello boy, who's a good boy then,' of someone who was missing his own dog perhaps.

He introduced himself as Dave and offered us a cup of tea. We went into the kitchen and I was having second thoughts about the tea and indeed the cup. The state of the kitchen was something I will not inflict on the reader, especially if you have eaten recently. Let's just say 'student kitchen' and leave it at that.

The tea was surprisingly good if I didn't look at the cup.

"The others will be back soon, they are just getting pizza." I didn't know why it took three of them. Perhaps one got the pizza and the other two rode shotgun.

The pizzas were two Margaritas, a Sloppy Giuseppe and an American Hot. I assumed the four had ordered one each but in fact they shared all the pizzas between them. They even offered some to Micah, Barker and myself. We declined. Well I declined on Barker's behalf but he started hoovering up any lost food from the floor. That must have been the only hoovering which had gone on in that room by the looks of it. I was only pleased they had the sense not to use that plague pit of a kitchen.

Dave introduced them to us.

"Big" Dave was only so-called to differentiate him from the almost identically-sized Dave. Like Dave, his subject was Physics. He was unshaven but then it was only 3 pm. He made a fuss over Barker who he also decided was a "good boy". If only he knew him when he was being a bad boy.

Sindy was in the uniform of tattered jeans, enhanced with air-holes for the knees. This was probably necessary as the knees were not scrupulously clean. She was afterwards described by Micah as "an airhead" which seemed unlikely as she was a Mathematics student but Micah seemed to have taken against her.

Maya completed the quartet. She smiled a lot. We were to discover that she was intermittently the inamorata of Dave, Big Dave and Sindy. She was the only one who didn't pay any rent.

Cans of the cheapest lager in the supermarket were produced and passed round. I made a mental note to bring a bottle next time when to my surprise, the ever-resourceful Micah produced one from her handbag. You could site a small town in her handbag and I had never got to the bottom of its variety of contents.

At length we talked about the day 'poor Miss Malapert' had died.

"Well I was cleaning the kitchen that day when the ambulance arrived," was the first piece of hogwash I heard. It was from Dave and I would swear nobody had ever cleaned that kitchen. My look must have conveyed as much because Maya put in her two-penn'orth.

"No, honestly, Dave really was cleaning the kitchen that day. I should know because it was my turn but he offered to do it for me. He is such a sweetie." This was delivered with a winning smile in Dave's direction.

"Those two," and here Maya's smile vanished, "were having a row in big Dave's bedroom."

"How do you know? The bedroom is two floors above the kitchen." I put in.

"Because I was in my room, silly. Though I expect everyone in the street could hear them, they were having a row and making a row if you see what I mean."

"Then how did you know Dave was in the kitchen?"

"Well, he texted me to say he was cleaning the kitchen." She looked at me as if I was particularly stupid.

I kept to myself the thought that a text could have come from anywhere.

"So Dave, you were in the kitchen." Micah put in, notebook in hand.

"I said so didn't I?" said Dave.

"Maya was in her room and Dave and Sindy, can you confirm you were in Dave, I mean Big Dave's, room?"

"Yes." They were almost in unison.

"What was the row about?"

"None of your business."

"Of course not, but we are treating Miss Malapert's death as suspicious so anything you can tell us which might help would be very useful."

"You? Who the hell are you to investigate suspicious deaths?" Sindy wanted to know.

"Well as we told Dave," We had told Dave nothing but Micah correctly assumed he had a memory like a goldfish, "we are private investigators."

Micah had printed off impressive cards for the pair of us with photo ID and an official-looking signature. You had to look close to see it was mine. These we produced. Although the atmosphere had cooled somewhat the students were still up for answering questions albeit in a surly way.

"So, this row, was it a secret?" I asked.

"Well hardly," said Maya, "or they wouldn't be telling the street about it."

I gestured to Maya to stay out of this and looked at Sindy again. However, it was Big Dave who answered.

"Well look it was something and nothing really. It was an argument, or perhaps a heated discussion, about feminism. Whether I classed as a male chauvinist pig for example." Big Dave essayed a grin at this, to indicate that of course, it wasn't true.

Sindy agreed about the nature of the argument but the look on her face said it came as a surprise to her that that was the substance of the row. Micah just wrote "MCP?" in her notebook.

We talked about "poor Miss Malapert" and Sindy said something quite interesting.

"She was a dear, really. When we were having a party, we told her as she was our only neighbour. I said that I hoped the noise wouldn't disturb her. She said there was no problem because she wouldn't hear it because she was deaf. She was very nice about it."

"When was this party?"

"Last weekend. We have a party most weekends. You know all work and no play makes Sindy a dull girl and all that."

On our way back we passed Miss Malapert's house and the boarded up property next to hers. We both noticed a light through the incomplete boarding which was swiftly extinguished. Clearly, we would have to look into Miss Malapert's other neighbours too.

The following day we dined at the John Selden. The improvement was noticeable. We could take Barker with us because not only was it a dog-friendly place but he was fed with dog biscuits by the staff. The portions were generous. I had the pensioner's lunch which was a large serving of beef with more vegetables than you could shake a stick at. It was quite enough for the two of us and nobody raised an eyebrow when we asked for two sets of cutlery despite the fact that Micah is not a pensioner.

The Cabernet Sauvignon was not Casillero del Diablo but it was very good. I may confess that I have never found a Cabernet Sauvignon I didn't like except on those rare occasions when bar staff have tried to pour me a Sauvignon Blanc. That didn't happen at the John Selden.

Its other advantage was that it was quite close to what I had come to think of as Malapert Terrace. We had arranged for the nephew, Matthew Malapert to let us into Miss Malapert's house. It had that smell which seems to cling around the dwellings of the old. We got used to it rapidly and hardly noticed it as we looked around the rooms. Matthew assured us they were unchanged since Miss Malapert's demise.

While Micah trawled through the paperwork I went with Matthew to the room where Miss Malapert had died. There were no signs of a struggle but then I would have expected even Doctor Winter to have noticed that. The smell was stronger in this room than any other and I suspected Miss Malapert spent a lot of time here.

The window had a good view of the street and I noticed a powerful set of binoculars. Matthew lightly referred to his aunt as "The Neighbourhood Watch". There was also a perfectly good medical stethoscope. I did a quick calculation and worked out that the wall of the bedroom was right next to Big Dave's room. The houses were of very similar construction.

An "Aha!" from Micah sent us back downstairs. She was holding a letter with a Specsavers' logo.

"Deaf my foot. She was only saying that to avoid a confrontation with any of her neighbours about the noise of the party. Her hearing was remarkably good for a woman of her age."

I told her about the stethoscope and her only comment was, "It beats holding a glass against the wall."

I asked Matthew if all the houses in the terrace had been built on the same pattern. He said that was probably the case but he actually didn't know. He then offered me a glass of whisky and Micah a cup of tea. We swapped.

Our next call was the house next door. Matthew knew nothing about the previous occupants.

"And the present occupants?"

"The place is deserted."

"Yes," I said, "but we saw a light there last night. It was extinguished as soon as we saw it. "

Miss Malapert's back garden had a gate which led to the back alleyway. As I had hoped, all of the houses in the terrace had a similar gate. I took a screwdriver to the back door of Miss Malapert's neighbour.

"Isn't that breaking and entering?" Micah asked.

"Technically, you're right but this is supposedly an empty house. Now, will you just hold that torch still for a minute while I get on with this?"

The back door was not a serious challenge and I had it opened in a few minutes. I then went on to make what could have been my last mistake.

I walked into the dark house but unfortunately, I ran straight into the resident who was less than pleased about the intrusion.

If you want to know what being hit over the head with a blunt instrument is like, I am here to tell you it is a lot less fun than it sounds.

I felt a pain. I saw a flash of light and the next thing I knew I was in casualty with Micah sitting in a chair by the bed looking worried.

"That's another fine mess you've gotten yourself into."

I tried to laugh. It hurt.

"I followed you into the house with the torch. God only knows why you went in without it. The resident had fled. They left a pickaxe handle."

"Not much point in going to the police."

"Not unless you want to be done for breaking and entering. The squatter could claim they were only defending their own property against a burglar."

"The Oscar Pistorius defence?"

"Think yourself lucky they didn't have a gun then."

I eventually saw a doctor after eight hours in A and E. He clearly thought I was wasting his time. Micah's story that I had walked into a door didn't convince him. He thought Micah and I had had a difference of opinion and she had belted me one.

"You'll live but you might like to buy yourself some paracetamol if your head bothers you. And don't row with any stroppy doors, eh."

The John Selden were used to us using their bar as our office. How many offices have a bar, excellent food and biscuits for Barker? Barker is a German Shepherd but I always think of him as an Alsatian. He is quite used to dozing under the table while we work.

"So Miss M used her stethoscope to listen to her neighbours. Big Dave and Sindy were having a row. We do not believe the story they spun us about the subject of the row." Micah said all this rapidly as she made notes.

"Do you think they killed her because she overheard the row? And what could it have been about to make them want to kill her?"

"Well. Firstly, they didn't know she wasn't deaf so didn't know she overheard them. Secondly, if Maya is telling the truth the ambulance arrived at the same time as the row. So Miss M had been dead for some time before the row."

"As for the subject of the row," I answered my own question, "They could have been rowing about something mildly illegal like drugs and thought they shouldn't tell us that."

"Well," Micah said, "I could smell cannabis in the kitchen. I thought that was par for the course for a student house."

"You could smell cannabis over all the other smells in that kitchen? Well done."

"I think our next port of call will be the house where I got this impressive bruise."

"Craig, you cannot be serious."

"Well we can go in daylight and forewarned is forearmed."

"I've got a bad feeling about this."

"Isn't that what Han Solo said?"

"Yes and look what happened to him."

"Look, Micah, I'll go on my own."

"Like hell, you will. If you go, I go. OK?"

I smiled at that. We finished our drinks, awakened Barker and set off for Malapert Terrace.

The back door of Miss Malapert's mysterious neighbour was still open after my ministrations with a screwdriver the previous day. There was no sign of the neighbour, though. Barker had a good sniff around and found some scraps in the kitchen which pleased him but did not take us much further forward.

Upstairs were the signs of a makeshift bedroom which had been abandoned rapidly. There was a filthy mattress on the floor, a glass, several bottles and most interestingly a mobile phone. We liberated the phone and with a quick look round the other rooms, which seemed unoccupied, we left for home.

Micah got to work on the phone. It took the FBI a week to crack the code on an iPhone. Micah used her dark arts to get into this one in an hour while I made tea and tried to make myself useful in the kitchen.

I took two ham sandwiches into the living room in time for Micah to shout "Eureka!"

Micah started with the deleted text messages. It seemed our friend (although a pickaxe handle over the head suggests a lack of friendship to me) was called David Jones. Most surprising of all the facts about David Jones – apart from all the jokes about lockers among his texts – was that he had a job. There were work texts from the shop where he worked.

Davies and Co was a small high street shop of the kind which Worthing has in abundance. It is an old-fashioned gents outfitters.

"That certainly doesn't sound like the job for a scruffy squatter, does it?"

"How do we know he is scruffy?"

"Well, you saw that bedroom. It didn't scream sartorial elegance to me,"

We finished our coffee and sandwiches and set off to Davies and Co. Mr Davies had inherited the old shop from his father. It had been founded by his grandfather. It was kept open by pride rather than business acumen. Mr Davies was losing money hand over fist and expected he would be unable to hand over the business to his son.

"Your son?"

"Well it's just as well that I have never had one, isn't it?"

He had nothing but praise for young David. He had taken to the business and was keen to learn from Mr Davies' experience. He couldn't give us his address but when I ventured to suggest the address of the squat he actually laughed.

"No. I don't think young David would be seen dead in that neighbourhood."

Well, we only had a couple of hours to wait for the man himself to arrive for work. We adjourned to a local cafe to wait. I don't know if there is such a thing as too much coffee but we have never yet reached that milestone. The lattes were not quite up to the standard of the Black Cat but they were perfectly acceptable.

We discussed how we should handle David Jones.

"Hit him over the head with a blunt instrument?"

"No, I think we may have to be a little more subtle than that." Micah said.

"Well, we could tell him we know his real address. By the by, I was thinking Miss Malapert's stethoscope might well have been used to eavesdrop on him." I said.

"He talked to himself?"

"He might have had company."

In the end, Micah's plan was probably the best one.

"David, I believe this is your phone."

David was clearly delighted and very surprised.

"How did you, what did you, where did you find it?"

"Where did you lose it?" Micah said.

"I didn't lose it. It was stolen from me by a scallywag. The man looked more like a tramp than anything else. I was calling for a taxi and this guy ran up and just snatched it out of my hand. The bastard. I have to say you could smell him before you saw him. He was wearing a stinking old brown coat and I suspect his shoes had seen better days. I gave chase but he was quick. Also, he knew the back-alleys around these parts so he was able to evade me. The fearful oik."

"What did he smell of, if you don't mind me asking?"

"Well it was an unwashed sort of smell. Come to think of it, it was mixed up with beer and tobacco. Not a holy trinity by any means, more an unholy one."

"We think he has been in a place where he couldn't wash for some time." I said mildly.

"I believe you. And thanks for getting my phone back. I can get a new phone but all the information on this one – numbers and addresses and what have you – would take an age to replace.

"But," he thought for a moment, "you're not the police. I reported the missing phone to the rozzers a week ago and they didn't seem particularly interested."

"Well they have a lot on their plate and they have taken their share of public sector cuts and all that."

"You're not making excuses for them are you?" he asked.

"No, we are just returning your phone."

"Well thank you. He produced a twenty-pound note. I was all for turning it down. Micah, on the other hand, took a different attitude. She also took the twenty with a smile. After all, she explained later, young Matt Malapert wasn't exactly paying us a fortune to investigate Miss Malapert's death.

"We ought to have a scale of fees. Research the market and all that sort of thing."

Micah sighed, "You mean I ought to research the market and draw up a scale of fees."

"That would be very good of you. Retrieving an iPhone should certainly be more than a twenty for a start."

"Well, at least we can cross David Jones from our list."

"Consign him to the briny deep you mean?"

Micah gave a watery smile and nodded.

We returned to the student house. We were to return there a number of times. They were hospitable. There was not a pickaxe handle in sight. The fact we always brought a bottle probably helped.

I could see no reason not to tell them about the missing phone and Miss Malapert's other neighbour. I was very pleased I had.

Maya told us a story about her phone going missing and then finding it down the back of the sofa. I looked at the sofa. It took some courage to put her hand down there I must say.

"And then, of course, the battery was flat. I had to use Sindy's charger to bring it back to life and she made such a fuss about me taking it while she was out at some boring Mathy sort of thing. I mean she wasn't using it was she? And then as soon as it was up and running the texts that had been waiting for weeks ('Days,' said Sindy with an unfriendly tone) arrived and it was like all 'Ping, ping, ping, ping.'"

When Maya had quite finished pinging, Sindy spoke quietly, "You know Maya is not American don't you?"

"But what about the accent? And she talks about Math not Maths." Micah said.

"Yes. She picked all that up from watching TV. She had boxed set after boxed set of bloody 'Friends' and she used to insist on us all watching them. She even watched them in the bedroom if you please. Some lover she was! Not that we were together for long, you understand. Too much 'Friends' and not enough friendship. She borrowed my stuff incessantly and sometimes didn't give it back at all. Technically, mind you I only mean technically, I wouldn't fall out with Dave's girlfriend, it was stealing."

"Got all the stuff back now?"

"Well yes, but I got it back from Dave, not Miss America."

It was the mention of Miss Malapert's neighbour which elicited the most useful response, however. Mind you Micah did put 'klepto?' next to Maya's name in her notebook.

"Oh, you mean Boo." Dave said and the others agreed and laughed.

"Like Boo Radley in *To Kill a Mockingbird*. He gives us all the creeps."

"He's been described as a scallywag," Micah offered, "that's something between a ne'er-do-well and a ragamuffin," she added by way of elucidation.

"Yes he's definitely one of those," said Big Dave, "'scruff', my mother would have said. A brown coat which has never been washed and a lingering aroma of tobacco, Tennants and BO."

"What you don't seem to know is that he was the original tenant, lived there with his wife. I don't know how she put up with him. He would roll up drunk in the early hours. Just as well old Malapert was deaf because it would have wakened the dead. The rows they had! We could hear them and I bet Maya could have heard them from the next street as she has exceptional hearing." He looked at Maya and it was not a friendly look.

She left the room and the others seemed to relax. That included Dave who was her current lover.

"Anyway," Big Dave continued, "she left him, taking the kids with her. I know about it because he was shouting obscenities from an upstairs window. Not the sort of thing to bring her back in a hurry. It was shortly after that that we heard Boo – real name Bob Iddy – was evicted for non-payment of rent and failure to maintain the property. He and all his stuff were just pitched into the street and he went off to drown his sorrows. I think they were three-quarters drowned already."

"What happened to his stuff?"

"Same thing as happens to anything which isn't nailed down in this street. It was nicked. Some 'scallywags' pitched up in a van and bundled it all in. Boo did his tiny nut when he found out. Then he broke into the boarded-up house and stayed there rent free. It's been three months now."

Micah, Barker and I held a meeting in the Black Cat. We banished the thought of the student kitchen with a lovely latte in a clean cup and one of their famous all-day breakfasts. Micah produced her notebook.

"How do we spell that guy's name?"

I hazarded a guess and she laughed. "Bibbedy Bobbidy Boo". We got some funny looks when she started singing,

"Salaca doo la menthicka boo la bibbidi-bobbidi-boo

Put 'em together and what have you got?

Bibbidi-bobbidi-boo!"

She wrote his name on her list of suspects. She added Bob because his alibi was a text which could have originated anywhere, for example next door. And his kitchen cleaning was questionable too. I got her to add Maya because although we only had her word to alibi the others, she had no alibi herself.

"Of course if we distrust Klepto Maya then that calls into question all the other residents."

Micah wearily added all of the names to her list.

"And Matt Malapert."

"Now, Craig, that is ridiculous. He was the only person who questioned Miss Malapert's death. I'll put him in for completeness but really this isn't an episode of 'Midsomer Murders.' "

"It is more like an Agatha Christie device. In two of her stories the narrator is the murder and in two others 'the butler done it.'"

Micah ordered another latte and after a fractional hesitation I joined her.

Micah looked at her list of suspects.

"I think Big Dave and Sindy alibi each other unless they both did it. I suppose that is possible." she said, "Maya steals," she continued after a pause, "but as far as we know she only steals from her friends or lovers."

"What if she stole from Miss Malapert and Miss Malapert caught her?"

"She received Dave's text about the kitchen."

"The kitchen nobody cleaned."

"No. Not ever as far as I could judge," Micah conceded.

"Maya could have received the text anywhere but she did know that Big Dave and Sindy were rowing."

"She could have heard that row chez Malapert if it were as loud as she claimed it was."

"Moving on, can we find out about Boo's known associates?" I asked.

"Why?"

"Well unless he talked to himself, Miss Malapert could not have overheard him."

"We don't know she did."

"No but known associates would give us some background on Bibbidy Bobbidy which might be very useful."

"You want me to hack the police national computer. That is a big deal, Craig."

"But you can do it."

"Leave it with me. You know flattery will get you everywhere with me." Micah smiled.

So did I.

While Micah was doing things with the computer, I had a chat on the telephone with Matt Malapert.

"You will know why I am asking this, Matt, so you won't be offended."

"No," he said uncertainly.

"Who was Miss Malapert's heir?"

"Well surely you know. I am."

"What do you inherit."

"Well that is the funny thing about it. I inherit the house of course. Between you and me there is not much prospect of selling the damned thing for a reasonable price. However, my aunt had a fair amount of money. The thing is, I can't find any savings books or account statements."

"Have you looked under the mattress?"

"Nothing but dust bunnies and that smell you remarked upon."

"So that is a mystery."

My phone buzzed at this point and I glanced at the text. It was from Dave. It simply read "Boo back" with the characteristic brevity and lack of punctuation of a text message.

"Matt," I said, "if you are having a job finding a buyer for your aunt's place, I suppose you wouldn't mind if Micah and I camped out there for a few days?"

"Not at all."

"Just don't tell anybody about it."

"Who would I tell?"

"Nobody, Matt, nobody at all."

The next thing was to make arrangements for Barker. We couldn't put him in kennels but his propensity to bark at the wrong moment might be an embarrassment during our sojourn in Malapert terrace.

I made another phone call.

"Dorothy, my favourite daughter."

"Stop right there, dad. I am your only daughter and you only ever say that when you want something."

"I want something."

"I knew it. Come on then, spit it out."

"Could you possibly look after Barker for a couple of days."

"Well I would love to but I do have to go out to work, you know. I expect you have forgotten what work is with your gold-plated pension."

"The gold plating is running a little thin but I could still manage a few bob to pay for a dog walker and you would be doing me a favour."

"I will be wanting dinner out when I return him."

"So we have a deal?"

"Yes when will you be bringing him here?"

"This afternoon."

"I am not working this afternoon so that would do fine."

When we arrived at the Malapert house, Micah immediately proceeded to banish the old-lady smell with a burst of Haze. It was their "spring flowers" variety. It smelt nothing like spring flowers but the room smelt a lot better than before.

Then she unpacked her equipment. She had clearly raided Maplin to obtain her array of microphones which were likely to be more efficient than Miss Malapert's stethoscope. They were linked wirelessly to her laptop. She had also brought enough food to feed the Eighth Army in case we got a little peckish.

We settled down to wait but the four sound-wave displays from the four mikes soon lost their charm. At this point Micah produced a pack of cards. 'Resourceful' could have been her middle name. We were happily ensconced on the now odour-free bed playing rummy when the first microphone detected a noise.

We decided that young Maya was not kidding about the amount of noise Big Dave and Sindy managed to make when they had a row. We could hear angry voices but only the mikes could pick up actual words.

"But it's your turn to clean the kitchen. You could pick up that bloody lasange for a start."

"What bloody lasagne?"

"The lasagne you dropped on the kitchen floor a week ago. You were as drunk as a skunk and you just left it lying there. We have been having to step round it."

"And nobody thought of moving it?"

"Why should anybody move it? It was your lasagne. It just got mouldier and mouldier and it is your turn to clean it up."

That is just a sample of the row. It went on for some time and I concluded that no lasagna was going to be cleaned up any time soon.

Micah filled me in on Boo's known associates or associate to be precise.

"The police have very little on Boo. They have him down as "of no fixed abode" which we know to be untrue. He was clearly unhappy living on the street and came back home. His crime sheet is very light. There were a few cases of petty larceny in his teenage years and the police were called to this house once when the neighbours (read Miss Malapert) complained about a row in which he offered to skin his wife alive. He claimed it was a joke and his wife backed him up at the time."

"His drinking companion is one Jack Low. The police have a lot on Jack Low. Robbery with violence seems to be a hobby with him and it is just possible that he has got Boo into bad habits."

Another microphone came to life. We did not know Boo's voice so we could not initially differentiate which was Jack and which was Boo except from the content.

"Jack, how the devil have you been?"

"Mustn't grumble." came the reply of a man who, I suspect, grumbled a lot. My needle-sharp brain identified him as Jack Low.

There was a sound of cans being opened and they settled down to a chinwag. They talked a lot about football which was terra incognita to Micah and myself but the laptop faithfully recorded it anyway.

Then came a statement which made both of us sit up.

"Who would have thought the old lady had so much money?"

"Well it wasn't all that much."

"How much was it then?"

"Well that's none of your business is it?"

"What about my share?"

"Oh you'll get what's coming to you all right. Now what say we open another can?"

"But you promised I would get half."

"Half? Why half? I had to do all the dirty work."

"How dirty was it, exactly?"

There was a laugh.

"No, no, no there was nothing like that. I just had to befriend the old biddy. I think she just wanted company. I know people like that and I know what to say to them."

"Like what?"

"I found out all about her family, there is basically just a nephew and she had plenty of criticism of him. He drank, though mind you she often had gin on her breath. She said he played the horses, unsuccessfully. Everybody plays the horses unsuccessfully. Horses never bet on human races, they're too smart. She went on that he never visited which was just not true but she didn't remember that he'd been. "

"Getting a bit doolally was she?"

"A bit, you say. No she was as mad as a box of frogs. Some days she thought that I was her nephew and then she'd have to tell me off for all my drinking and my gambling for hours on end. And at other times she thought that I was her cousin Edgar, who came from South Africa and I had to play along and pretend that Apartheid was still going strong and Mandela was still on Robben Island. She was fundamentally a fruit cake.

"She trusted me so much that she gave me a key to the house if you can believe it. You know, I really think that if I had waited long enough then she would have just handed the money over to me, thinking I was St Peter or something."

"So why didn't you wait?"

"Ah. I'm impatient that's my trouble. Just like I'm impatient for you to get on and open that beer. Now get a move on, there's a good boy.

"I'll tell you this, though. I enjoyed putting the pillow over her face almost as much as I enjoyed the spondulix. I wouldn't have to worry about her constant rabbit, rabbit, rabbit. She could talk for England if it were an Olympic Sport. On and on and on. The same routine often like a broken record."

"Now what were you saying about my cut?"

"Oh your cut is it? You want a cut? I'll give you a cut."

There was the sound of a struggle. This was followed by a scream which ended in a liquid sort of gurgle and then there was silence.

We just looked at each other, quite stunned. For all we knew we had just witnessed a murder. Micah silently indicated her intention to call the police. She tried various parts of the room but eventually she went into the corner where the best mobile reception could be found. This move on her part might very well have saved our lives.

We were suddenly aware of footsteps in the house. Then, after a pause, there were footsteps coming up the stairs. I put out the lights but the staircase lights came streaming in under the door after our visitor had turned them on.

I swear that the man who opened the door was as surprised as I was. He had in his hand a blood-stained knife but he was clearly not expecting to find anybody in the house. We later discovered that he was going to gut the mattress to see if there was any more money which he had missed on his previous visit.

A knife however is no match for a vacuum cleaner which has been thrown with deadly accuracy. He had not noticed Micah and of course he couldn't be aware of her athletic prowess. I don't know if tossing the hoover is a regular activity at her gym but she was very good at it.

The man went down like a sack of potatoes and Micah sat on him. She reached for his throat as if to throttle him.

"No need to strangle the suspect." I said from the bed.

"I am taking his pulse. He is still alive. I can't say the same for Boo. I think Jack Low has killed him."

We waited for the police to arrive. It took them about three-quarters of an hour. Then of course we had to explain to them twice what was going on before they summoned up the energy to have a look next door. The constable who had been left to guard us was surprised to hear his colleague's voice coming from Micah's laptop. Modern technology was a bit of a closed book to him – a closed notebook certainly.

"I am going to need a crime scene investigation team here ASAP," was all his colleague managed to get out before he threw up very loudly. The sight of Boo after he was cut up was even less preposessing then when he was alive and kicking.

The police confiscated Micah's laptop and mikes. She made sure that she got a detailed receipt but they insisted that the laptop would be needed for the trial. They would keep it for several months. Micah later discovered they had installed Candy Crush on it and had a leader board of winning scores.

"You can't just backup the MP3s?" she asked.

"MP3s is it, little lady, MP3s. No politicians here, darlin'." was all the reply she got.

We were at the police station for six hours making statements and having them laboriously written out by someone who looked as though he didn't quite know what a pen was for but was suspicious of it anyway on general principle.

And that was that. They didn't even offer us a cup of tea: public spending cuts, you see. Jack Low was eventually tried and he went down for life on two counts of murder. The judge in this "particularly vile case of the murder of a harmless old lady for her money" did say that in Jack Low's case 'life' should mean life, not 20 years.

We had to go and tell the students all about it of course. We thought it wise to omit any reference to eavesdropping on their conversations. While I regaled the four of them with the tale of how Miss Malapert had met her fate, Micah descended on the kitchen wearing a smog mask and wielding every kitchen-cleaning fluid known to man. The next time we visited, of course, the kitchen had reverted to type.

Body in the Kitchen

"There is a corpse in our kitchen!"

"For a family of vegetarians that must be quite unusual."

Micah's tongue does run away with her at times and she knows the Carter family have zero sense of humour. I took the phone from her firmly, she snatched it back.

"So tell me all about it, Joe." she said with a look at me which sent me off to sit down and think about my behaviour.

"That's about it."

"Well male or female? Probable cause of death?"

"Just a tick, I'll have a look."

There was a pause.

"Male, female come to think of it, but you know, wearing trousers."

"Men's trousers or women's trousers?"

"Oh. What is the difference?"

Micah thought about this.

"Well what size are they?"

"Just a tick. 32-34 but it is definitely a woman."

"Wearing trousers made for a man."

"If you say so."

"Would it be a good idea if we came round to have a look or have you called the police?"

"Why would I call the police?"

"You have a corpse in your kitchen."

"Well technically. I will report the finding to the police as and when I discover the body."

"Which will be?"

"Shall we say tomorrow."

"Tomorrow?"

"I don't go into the kitchen that often. Can you two come over and just, you know, have a look around?"

So we sort of went round to have a look.

The body was face down on the kitchen floor. The skin was cold to the touch and there was no pulse in the carotid artery. Although the woman in man's trousers was clearly dead there was no visible sign of the cause of death.

In addition the clothes had no pockets and there were no name tags or anything to identify the poor woman.

We went into the living room where Joe had made us a cup of tea.

"Didn't you go into the kitchen to make the tea?"

"Ah, hadn't thought about that."

"Well I hope you don't make a slip-up like that with the rozzers. I suggest you call them sooner rather than later. They can do all the forensic flapdoodle and find out how the corpse met her end, who she was and things like that."

"I mean she can't have died from eating your cooking, can she?" Micah asked but got no reply.

Joe took the tea things back into the kitchen after he had agreed to ring the police tout suite. Then he actually screamed.

We rushed to the kitchen to find what the screaming was all about.

The corpse had vanished.

"The door handle has been wrenched off." said Micah. She didn't need to mention the obvious point that it had been wrenched off *from the inside.*

Joe was just relieved that he didn't have to call the police. There was a fair amount of portable property of dubious provenance around the house and the police have a habit of asking awkward questions.

And that would have been that apart from a curious coincidence the following week. I was walking Barker in the recreation ground when I saw a woman sitting on a bench. She was apparently asleep. As soon as I saw her face in profile I recognised her. Here was the mysteriously mobile corpse from the Carter kitchen.

I looked around. The rec is usually quite busy with dog-walkers and dogs but I was in luck. Barker and I and the lady were the only ones around. I sat down beside the woman and Barker stretched himself out on the grass. He was dog-tired.

The woman was dressed in similar but not identical clothes to the corpse. I noticed that the pockets were sewn up and she didn't have a handbag. What struck me most of all was that she was definitely not breathing.

For a moment I had a crazy idea that someone had moved the corpse, possibly keeping it in a freezer, only to move it again to this location. Instead of a decent burial the woman was perhaps doomed to tour the town. I was itching to find out if her skin was cold and her pulse non-existent. On the other hand I didn't want to look like an old perv.

I moved to another bench and ostentatiously read the newspaper. I couldn't for the life of me tell you what the news was that day because, let's face it, this was an intriguing situation.

My wait was rewarded. Without a yawn or a stretch the woman stood up and started to walk across the rec.

Barker is as good at following a suspect as I am. Truth to tell he is rather better. We followed the very alive corpse through the winding roads and twittens of Durrington. She seemed to know them very well. Unlike footpaths anywhere else, the twittens are usually concealed by hedges and look as if they lead to someone's house. It is easy to make a mistake. She didn't make any.

At length she arrived at a house. I made a note of the number as I walked past. She didn't have a key but she rang the bell and was let in by a man. I later discovered from the electoral roll that his name was Mr Grey and he lived apparently alone in the house. If it is possible to talk about a human being as 'nondescript' then Mr Grey fitted the bill. He was instantly forgettable.

The electoral roll gave me an idea, however. I got Micah to put together a redding card as used by genuine pollsters which showed the inhabitants of Mr Grey's street. She dutifully went from door to door asking about the voting intentions of the inhabitants and then trying to engage them in chit chat about the other residents. One or two warned her off approaching Mr Grey or the Professor of Surliness as one called him.

When she got to Mr Grey's door he said a rude word and shut the door in her face. However if Mr Grey was taciturn to the point of rudeness his neighbour, Mrs Hughes, was garrulous in the extreme.

Not only did Mrs Hughes tell Micah all about Mr Grey she also told her about the doings of everyone in the street. She appeared to be titillated and scandalised in equal portions by all the 'goings on' that were going on.

"Charles Grey is a surly old curmudgeon. That's all there is to it. Of course he was different when she was there. His wife that is, Mary. She ran off with a golfing instructor." She added the last in a hushed whisper. "I hear say she's come back to the old devil but it doesn't seem to have made him any less grumpy. He had a good job before he retired. Something to do with freezin' people when they died until a cure could be found for what ailed them. A bit creepy if you ask me. Anyway won't you come in for a cup of tea love."

The tea came with a lot more information, none of it relevant to the case.

Meanwhile I consulted my old friend Google about our Mr, I should actually say Professor, Grey. He was not involved in Cryogenics at all, Mrs Hughes had the wrong end of the stick. He was a professor of cybernetics.

It was just possible that there was the clue to the curious incident of the corpse in the kitchen. What if Professor Grey had found a substitute for his errant wife in the realms of robotics?

I made a visit to Professor Grey. I said I was working for the New Scientist and wanted a talk with 'Mrs Grey'. I said that so the inverted commas were apparent. I think Professor Grey was confident his robot could pass for human in conversation. However there is one question the Turing Test, a test to show whether you are talking to a human or a machine, does not use.

As soon as Mrs Grey walked in, I asked it. After that she was happy to explain her unexpected appearance in the Carter's kitchen. The Prof's house backed on to the very similar Carter residence. She had made a simple mistake which would never happen again. She needed to recharge, lying on the kitchen floor would fit the bill. As soon as she was recharged, she went to leave but some idiot had locked the back door. She wrenched off the handle, she didn't know her own strength. She smiled sweetly at that. I made an excuse and left.

"So that is the explanation. She wasn't dead. She had never been alive. But what was the question?" Micah asked

"'Are you a robot?' You see the Prof was very stupid for a clever man. He hadn't programmed her to lie."

"What do we do now?"

"Nothing. He hasn't broken any laws and he seems happy with his Stepford Wife."

"It is about time he took her shopping for some new clothes." said Micah, practical as ever.

Norm

It is surprising how diminishing it can be to shorten a name. "Norman" is a good noble name. It is applied to a whole region in France and of course to the conquest of England. "Norm" on the other hand was a whining weasel of a man and he was standing in my office.

"It's like this, Mr McLary," he whimpered apologetically, "There's been a total miscarriage of justice and I won't stand for it. I won't."

I knew he would get to the point eventually so I toyed with my notepad to give the impression I would like to write something down.

"You see, it's like this," ("WHAT is like WHAT?" I almost shouted but possessed my soul with patience.)

"I'm not saying my brother Tony was a saint. No he wasn't a saint. He was more of a ne'er-do-well if you are familiar with the expression. The number of times I've said to Tilly, that's my wife you understand, 'That Tony will come to a bad end.' Tilly is always one to be agreeable and in short she agreed with me. 'Yes, Norm,' she'd say, 'come to a bad end he will.'"

"Well to cut a long story short it was that Baker that caused all the trouble in the first place when he accused our Tony."

"Baker?" I asked.

"Yes, Mr Baker, he was a grocer. We used to laugh about that. 'He should have been a baker,' I'd say to Tilly and she'd agree of course. This Baker went and accused our Tony of shoplifting. Shoplifting, I ask you."

"Tony was not a saint, as I may have said before, but shoplifting, I ask you. You see if it comes to diddling the tax man or cheating at cards, well Tony's your man. I mean nobody likes the tax man do they? And folk that play cards for money, well they're asking to be taken to the cleaners aren't they?"

I took these questions to be rhetorical so I let Norm unfold the story in his own way.

"But shoplifting. I ask you. Well that was bad enough and Tony was taken in by the rozzers, perhaps I should say the police, seeing as how you're almost police yourself aren't you? Then that bloody Baker only goes and gets himself murdered with Tony's bloody razor. Excuse my French but it actually was bloody after Baker got himself murdered with it."

"And you would like us to clear your brother's name?"

"Exactly."

"On the charge of murder?"

"Well no, I can see Tony might have taken umbrage at Baker over the accusation, I mean I ask you. And Tony was always too ready with that razor of his. No, Mr McLary, I want you to clear his name of shoplifting."

I took myself off to Baker the Grocer while Micah, my partner in crime-fighting and the love of my life, interviewed Norm's long-suffering wife. It was just a guess on my part to say that she was long-suffering but it was not rocket science to realise that being married to Norm was not the answer to a maiden's prayer.

The sign above the door still read "Baker" and no doubt continued to cause confusion to customers unfamiliar with the shop. It was appropriate however as I was to find.

"I was very sorry to hear about Mr Baker's murder." I ventured as my mint humbugs were being wrapped for me.

"Nobody ain't murdered me!" The pimply youth behind the counter seemed never to tire of this rather tasteless joke.

"I'm Frank Baker Junior," he explained, still convulsed with mirth, "And I ain't dead. It's the old bastard you want and you can't have him because he's caught a bad case of death so he has."

"Are you still in mourning?" I asked.

"No to tell you the truth, I didn't know him. I was brought up (if you can call it that) by my old mum, Nadia Baker. She still kept the Baker name because her maiden name was Entiknap and people found Baker easier on the ear."

"Of course the old bastard, as she always called him, wouldn't leave his blessed shop to her. Then he found that he had nobody else to leave it to but me. Now she works here anyway. Here, Nadia, come and talk to this customer. He wants to give his consequences, I mean dolences obviously, condolences on the departure of the old bastard."

Nadia, who had a cigarette hanging from her lower lip in contravention of every rule of health and safety, came shuffling out of the back room.

There was just time for young Frank to warn me quite loudly, "You'll have to speak up because she's a bit deaf."

"And stupid," he added with a flourish of filial piety.

"What did you want, dear?"

"I WAS JUST ASKING AFTER OLD FRANK."

"There is no need to shout, young man, I can hear perfectly well. Now what was it you wanted. Did the old bastard owe you money?"

I am sorry but most of her conversation consisted of "The old bastard" this and "the old bastard that" and I had to conclude that the Bakers, both mother and son, did not have any useful information on either the shoplifting or the killing. If they were telling the truth (always a useful precautionary phrase in my job) they had not seen the old Baker for years and years.

There was just one piece of information which might be useful. There was a shop assistant, Amish, who had been employed below minimum wage by Frank Baker senior.

"I had to let him go," Frank confided, "you see Nadia is stupid enough to work for nuffink if you can believe it."

I could. I got Amish's address from Frank Junior. It turned out he was a Hamish Hamilton and lived in Durrington.

I met up with Micah in the John Selden and I summarised my lack of findings as we tucked into a steak and kidney pie which could have fed a small village. We always ordered for one with cutlery for two in the John Selden. We always took Barker because he could be sure of being spoilt with dog treats.

"Well the first thing was that Matilda, that's Tilly's name, took an instant objection to Barker and I had to leave him in the yard. I was worried he might eat one of the dog ends which littered the place and that would be his dog end so to speak."

Did I mention that Micah's jokes are actually worse than mine?

"I swept the blasted dog ends away from the drainpipe where I had to tie him up and this annoyed Matilda too. She thought I was one of those do-gooders who didn't want her to smoke and she 'wouldn't have none of it.' so there. I didn't like to say that I couldn't care less whether she harmed herself but I was protecting Barker. He's not as young as he was but he still had a puppy habit of eating everything in sight."

"So I got off to a bad start but eventually we settled down to a cup of tea at a table on which she put a tablecloth which was last washed at the same time as the Turin shroud. The tea cups were not much better although the tea was surprisingly good."

"The bacteria probably improved the flavour."

"That is not helpful, Craig," Micah said and took a long draught of Cabernet Sauvignon to take away the memory of the tea cup.

"So, Matilda?" I prompted.

"Call me Tilly" came from Micah's phone. These smart phones are wonderful. Nobody suspects a phone and Micah and I use them to record all our interviews. That might be illegal by the way so don't tell anybody.

"Now is it about Tony and his shoplifting activities? So-called activities I should say."

"Tell me about Tony," Micah said. The phone did not record a blush on Tilly's cheek when she said this but Micah had noted it.

"Well you know he's a bad 'un, Norm always says that and he should know seeing as how he's his brother. I think he cheats at cards. We would never play him for money no matter how many times he asked. He did have a certain charm but Norm says so do snakes though I don't think Tony was like a snake."

"What is he like?"

"Well he's a you-know bit of a ladies' man, well so Norm says anyway. I wouldn't know about that. Changing the subject, he was accused of shoplifting rubber gloves, a lot of them. Well Norm said, 'What the devil (he used a much naughtier word than 'devil') would Tony do with a hundred rubber gloves, cut them up for condoms?' He's a big joker is my Norm."

Micah stopped the recording.

"A lot of the rest of it was, 'Norm says this' and occasionally, 'Norm says that.' I think we will probably get more information from Tony himself.'

"Can we get in to see him?" I wondered.

"No," said Micah with a sweet smile, "but his lawyers can. And they have a secure computer network."

"You're not suggesting that you will use your dark arts on the computer."

"I already have."

"And..."

"Norm is not going to like it."

Micah looked around the John Selden but only Barker was paying any attention to us and he knows how to keep his mouth shut.

"Tony has a cast-iron alibi for the time of the murder. Grocer Baker shuffled off this mortal coil on the evening of 25th March as a result of a savage attack with a razor which was left on the premises but devoid of fingerprints or DNA evidence except the blood of the grocer. It happened between the hours of 7 and 9."

She paused again but I knew she would go on without any prompting from me.

"And between those hours, Tony can confirm that he was having intimate relations with a lady."

"And the lady?"

"Was Tilly of course. Norm was at the gas works while the brother was up to his monkey business."

"They have gas works these days?"

"He works for calor gas and they do a roaring trade. The lawyers have talked to Tilly and at first she denied everything. When the senior partner pointed out to her that any information could be held in reserve, treated confidentially and a pack of other lies, she changed her story. She didn't want people to think badly of her. At first she claimed they were playing Rummikub but on being pressed as to why she did this when her Norm was away from the premises she confided that it was strip Rummikub.

"She then had to sign an affidavit to the effect that she knew of her own knowledge that the suspect Tony Hodges was in her company during the hours when the offence was committed. It went straight to the police. They will not tell all this to Norm unless they need to put additional pressure on Tilly."

"Which means?"

"It will be all round Durrington by tea time."

"There is still the matter of the ownership of the cut-throat razor."

"Tony had several cut-throat razors and he was able to produce them. He was not bothered about the question of why he had so many. 'I keep losing 'em like dunn I" and there was no way to prove the provenance of the particular razor. The police insistence that it was Tony's was part of what I believe is called a fit-up."

"There is one thing about Tony's razors though. For all his insistence that he is always mislaying them he is very careful to clean them thoroughly after every time he uses one. So the lack of fingerprints is not in itself suspicious."

"So that's that. Who are our suspects then?"

Micah got out her notebook. She uses a paper notebook for lists of suspects and a computerised one for everything else. This is an eccentricity of hers based on reading too many Dorothy Martin murder mysteries.

She wrote down *Frank Baker*, she hesitated a moment and then wrote down *Nadia Baker*.

"What about 'amish 'amilton?" I asked.

"I'm not putting him down until you've interviewed him." Micah said firmly. She then added *Tony Hughes* to her list and then added *Tilly Hughes* for good measure.

"There is nothing so suspicious…"

"…as a good alibi." I completed.

Hamish Hamilton did not like Frank Baker Senior and hadn't a good word for Frank Baker Junior, unless you count "skinflint."

He concluded our brief interview with this summary, "You do realise that by getting himself murdered that old bastard cleared the way for the young bastard to take over? So I didn't have no motive. It cost me my job. Also I can show you my razor, it's electric. I never even used a cut-throat razor. I was down the Vintner's on the night in question. Anyone can vouch for me. I think that covers all your questions, Mr McLary."

"Call me Craig."

"No Mr McLary. You can take your suspicions and shove them…"

Well I don't need to draw a diagram of what he wanted me to do with them. I think it's a physiological impossibility anyway.

When I got back home, Micah was suspiciously cheerful. I related my interview with Hamish and she only seemed to be half-listening. Barker was all ears though. He was also all tongue, all over my hands.

"Can I bring you back to the question of the razor?" she asked.

"I thought we agreed that it couldn't be proven that it was Tony's."

"Yes but there was one person who thought that it could."

Micah waited for that to sink in.

"The person who did not have an alibi. The person who had good reason to try to frame Tony for the murder," she added in case my thought processes were particularly slow.

"Didn't have an alibi?"

"I did what the police should have done in the first place. Norm was at work during those hours but he was working alone. He could have slipped out at any time and done the deed. He knew about Tony's goings-on with Tilly and he was not having it."

"The other thing our Norm didn't know was that there was CCTV footage of him passing a shop which was between Baker's and the Gaz works at 8 pm and passing the same shop on the way back at 8.34 pm."

"How on earth do you know that?"

"I didn't but the police were kind enough to check for me after I tipped them off about Norm's lack of alibi. They are, I think the term is 'sweating', him now. I can't see our Norm standing up to pressure very well can you?"

Micah was right as ever. Norm started singing like a canary as the saying goes. Among other things he admitted to planting the rubber gloves under Tony's bed. His anger against Tony made Cain look like a desirable sibling. The police finally had the right Mr Hughes in custody.

Tilly lost no time in dissolving her marriage to the jailbird and moving in with the brother. The last time I saw her she was happy with the change in her circumstances. She confided that it was her idea for Norm to come and see me.

"He wasn't happy but at the time I didn't know why." she said with an ambiguous smile. Well she had precious little to smile about when she had the whining weasel as a life partner. I wished her all the best.

Mona

I was having a rant to Micah about one of my pet peeves in the bar of the John Selden.

"I don't understand why the post office has sent me a form to my address, which they obviously must know, asking me to fill it in with my address."

"Moaner!" is what I heard from the woman advancing towards me from the bar with an outstretched hand.

Micah snapped out of that glazed-over state she affects whenever I start off about people asking my address when they already know it, the BBC news including stories about BBC programmes as if they were news or just the Government in general.

The woman continued to advance towards me with her hand out, she even wiggled it as if she were impatient with me for some reason.

"Mona Sikes, Mr McLairy," she turned her beaming smile on Micah and added, "Mrs McLairy. They told me behind the bar as how you're one of those defectives."

"Detectives, Mrs Sikes, detectives."

"Well yes but they said as how you were defective in terms of clients so you would probably be cheap," she said with the same beaming smile which was beginning to get on my nerves. I caught Micah smirking which didn't improve matters.

Mona sat down with her port and lemon and immediately started on her story.

"I have been married to Tony for these thirty-five years. That's Tony Sikes." She looked at Micah who had taken out her notebook. Mona even spelt out the name for her and checked she had written it down correctly.

"Lately he's been acting queer. There ain't no two ways about it. Mrs Jones, that's my next door neighbour, Aretha Jones. Anyway, Mrs Jones, I call her Aretha myself but I wouldn't advise you to do that until you've known her for twenty or so years, young man. Aretha says to me, 'you mark my words,' it being a saying of hers, 'you mark my words you'll find a skirt at the bottom of it."

"So I take it your neighbour thinks Mr Sikes has been seeing another woman. Has she got any evidence?" asked Micah with her pen poised.

"No no no," Mona laughed, "she was just listening to what I says to her about Sikesy's goings on."

"For example."

"Oh, I like that, 'for example,' indeed. Well let me tell you, young man, there was never a better provider than my Sikesy but I found out quite by accident that he's been earning about twice what he told me. Now, what do you think about that?"

"What was this accident?"

"Well, I asked my mate Millie in confidence just how much her Edward earned since he has the same kind of job as Sikesy at the same firm and she told me. She also let slip that Sikesy earned the same when I seemed surprised. And that's not all. He keeps odd hours these days. He used to come home regular as clockwork at 6 o'clock and expect his dinner on the table or I'd get 'what for' I can tell you." She smiled fondly at the memory.

"Now he's back at all hours and," she looked around, "then there's the blood!"

Both Micah and I perked up at that remark. Micah looked a question at Mrs Sikes.

"Well you remember that old song, but you're too young I expect, 'Lipstick on your collar' it was called. Connie Francis used to sing it. I found what I thought was lipstick on my Tony's collar but when I looked closer I saw it was blood. HE said he cut hisself shaving but I'm not so sure."

"What happened to the shirt?"

"It went into the wash with everything ..else. Tony would soon know if one of his shirts went missing wouldn't he?"

"Anyway, Mr McLairy, I want you to find out what on earth Tony's been up to. I'll pay yer. How does ten pounds an hour sound?"

"It's fifty pounds an hour plus expenses."

"Fifteen."

"Twenty." Micah looked at me as if to suggest I had come down in price too quickly. Then she thought about the bills and decided this was better than no job at all.

I am a detective, no matter how poor and indeed cheap a detective Mrs Sikes might think I am. I can tail a suspect with the best of them. Or so I thought.

It started out quite well. I used a photograph which Mona had provided for me to pick Tony out from the employees leaving the office where he worked, "Macaroni Imports." I had ascertained that Macaroni was the name of the original owner rather than an indication of what they imported. Tony was a man of average height and as far as I could tell average everything else. He was in his mid-forties.

The shades of night were falling as Tony wended his way through some of the many twittens with which Worthing is gifted. I had to get closer to my suspect as the light was failing. This is always a tricky moment in sleuthing. In the event, I got so close to Tony that my face collided with his fist as I came incautiously round a corner.

Either he had decided I was following him or he was the sort of chap to engage in random acts of violence against strangers. I kept an open mind on that as well as an open lip and a grazed cheek. It would seem that Tony was one of those people who carry brass knuckles around with them 'just in case.'

The pavement was getting cold so I eventually picked myself up, dusted myself off and set off for home.

Micah was duly sympathetic and she offered Savlon externally and whisky internally for my condition. However, I could see that beneath her sympathy there was a suppressed excitement.

"So we have no way of knowing where Tony has gone," I said.

"I wouldn't say that." said Micah enigmatically.

I waited. I knew she would spill the proverbial beans eventually.

"You see Tony had a mobile phone. It was child's play to follow his movements."

Assuming the child had a working knowledge of computers and mobile networks I supposed that was true.

Micah brought up a map which was updated every minute. It showed the pinpoint which indicated Tony. It showed exactly where he was going.

After discouraging me from following him any further, he had apparently doubled back on his route and ended up at a surprising destination.

Micah said what I was thinking, "Why on earth would he walk out of the front entrance of Macaroni's only to sneak back in by the back way half an hour later?"

"I think our Sikesy is up to no good."

"What do we know about Macaroni Imports?"

"I have hacked into their computer system while you were out. It seems that they import electronic equipment from the far east. They evade tax on a massive scale but this is par for the course for any medium to large business. They transfer profits to their subsidiaries in Panama so they pay no tax on them in the UK. They are crooks but perfectly respectable crooks on the surface at least."

In the morning a distressed Mona was on the telephone.

"It's my Sikesy. He ain't never been out all bloody night before. I want to know what's become of him. Weren't you supposed to be follerin' him? So where the bloody hell is the little bastard?"

Finding the little bastard became our top priority. Micah consulted the oracle of her laptop and confirmed that his phone was still at Macaroni's but that didn't mean that Sikesy was. She tried ringing him to no avail.

Micah has the apparently illegal habit of listening in to police radio broadcasts. It might be illegal technically but it was very useful this time. As we took Barker for his morning walk she was tuned in on her phone and attending closely to the headphones.

"He's dead," Micah announced suddenly in the middle of Durrington Recreation Ground. I didn't have to ask who. "They have found the body and confirmed the identity. He died from a blow to the back of the head which was administered by the proverbial blunt instrument. He was alive when the paramedics arrived but the only words he said did not make much sense to them. 'Come for tea.' They thought it was an odd invitation under the circumstances."

"Do we have any evidence that the so-called 'little bastard' was a music lover?"

"None at all."

"So is it likely that he would be quoting from Handel's 'Messiah'?"

"Pardon?"

"The exact words are 'Comfort Ye' but they are easily mistaken."

"Handel's Messiah? Well that is a coincidence."

I waited for Micah to explain further.

"Would you care to guess what the police found in Sikesy's front room about five minutes ago?"

"Handel? The Messiah?"

"Close. There were something like a thousand CDs. Mona insisted that she bought them at car boot sales and just hadn't got around to buying a CD player. It seems likely our Sikesy was stealing them from his employer."

"Well that would have annoyed them but was it enough for them to want to kill him?"

"Probably not but the fact Mona lied to the police will be useful to us."

"Why would it help us?"

"It means the CDs are still in her front room. I think we should pay our former client a little visit if only to collect what she owes us."

"I 'spect you've come for your money. Well you can whistle for it. The old bastard won't be doing any of his philanthropising where he's going."

Micah and I both thought "philandering" and both decided to keep quiet.

"No, Mrs Sikes, we've come to offer our condolences on your loss."

Mona thought it was only proper to offer us a cup of tea.

"Look, Mr McLairy, I will pay yer for yer time but can you just wait until the insurance money comes through?"

"Don't you worry about that, Mrs Sikes."

"Mona, please."

Micah had already checked. The insurance money was roughly three thousand pounds. It was a lot of money but was it worth killing for?

While I was chatting with Mona, Micah had to visit the toilet. She was some time so I explained to Mona that Micah had a weak bladder. Mona was not only sympathetic but she decided to talk at some length about her own medical condition. Had I been a doctor I could have picked up a lot of useful information.

Micah eventually returned and we made our goodbyes. Mona wouldn't think of letting us go without a slice of cake wrapped in greaseproof paper.

I looked a question at Micah as we made our way home and Barker tucked in to the cake. By way of reply she opened her bag and showed me a CD. The Messiah.

"And was it the only copy in the front room?"

"Believe me, I checked. That is why I was so long answering a call of nature. Obviously you covered for me. Most of the CDs had their cellophane wrapping still on so that Sikesy could sell them on. As it is I imagine that is exactly what Mrs 'Call me Mona' Sikesy will be doing. She has no music in her soul."

"But do you think she killed the old bastard in revenge for his supposed infidelity?"

"That would be very strange behaviour for somebody who had hired the best detectives in Durrington to keep a beady eye on the erring soul."

I preened myself at the "best" label but Barker was unimpressed. A leaf he was intent on marking by peeing on it was much more important in his scheme of things.

Anticipating my next question, Micah suggested that our next move would be to convey our condolences to Tony's work-colleague, Edward.

"If something dodgy is going on he will be on edge. If whatever it was led to Tony's death he will be terrified."

...

"What are you? Some kind of alsatian?"

Edward "call me Eddie" Pearson was one of those people who prefer talking to Barker to talking to us. Well it breaks the ice. He disappeared off to the kitchen to find some treats. The packet said they were cat treats. Fortunately Barker cannot read.

"We were sorry to hear about the death of your friend."

"Which friend?"

"Tony Sikes."

"No friend of mine. I just knew him vaguely. We don't even work on the same floor. Sorry, mate, you've been misinformed."

"What is it like working for Macaroni's?"

"Well it's a job, that's all you can say for it. The money is quite good but Macaroni's think they own you body and soul. That would be the reason our Tony was ripping off the company."

He noticed our faces and added the word, "allegedly." Then he tried to smile. It was not a success. And that was the last word we got out of "call me Eddie".

As we were walking Barker home, Micah revealed that she had had better luck with Eddie's wife, Millie. As was her custom she had recorded the conversation on her phone.

"Eddie and Tony were thick as thieves. By which I mean they were good friends. My Eddie was never a thief. I am not so sure about Tony mind you. They fell out over a game of cards. Eddie accused Tony of cheating. I think the amount of money involved was two pounds or so but Eddie never liked losing."

"The same went for work of course. Macaroni's were losing markets to Thompsons. Thompsons seemed to have advance knowledge of the lines Macaroni would be importing. The things my Eddie said about Thompsons! Well, Mrs McLairy I wouldn't repeat them in front of a lady like yourself but you can take my word for it he didn't like losing out to them."

"Does Eddie go out much?" Micah asked innocently.

"What do you mean?"

"Well does he go down the pub for instance."

"I don't know what you're implicating I'm sure. He does go down the Dog and Rabbit some evenings, I mean he was there on Wednesday for instance. But you mustn't go thinking he drinks away the housekeeping. He's not like that. Not like that at all."

We decided to divide our forces. Micah was to tackle the Sikes's neighbour, Mrs Jones who we had been warned not to call "Aretha". I had an appointment with a dog and a rabbit.

I described Eddie to the landlord. He knew him all right. The only thing was, Eddie couldn't have been there on a Wednesday because it was Quiz Night and he wasn't into that sort of thing.

When I got home, I could tell straight away that Micah was excited about something. However she was methodical and started by playing the recording of her chat with Mrs Jones.

To cut a long story short, Mrs Jones only knew what Mona had told her. She had a splendid collection of speculations about what 'that bastard' had been up to but no facts at all.

"However..." There is something about the way Micah uses that word. It is always an introduction to a pertinent piece of information.

"Listen to this."

She put a CD into the laptop. The cacophony which came from it was a fair indication that it was a data CD not a music one.

"The Messiah played by an experimental electronic combo?" I ventured.

"No," Micah really was very pleased with herself, "It contains heavily protected data. Well I expect Sikesy thought it was heavily protected. I think a child of ten could have broken his encryption. It contained Macaroni's business plan for the financial year. Thompsons would pay a lot of money for this stuff."

We were interruped by a telephone call.

"Mr McLairy. Thank God. I've had an intruder. He came in through the window and he was fiddling around with my CD collection if you can believe it. I hit him over the head with a poker. I have got a nasty feeling he's dead."

"We'll be right there."

'Call me Eddie" was lying in a pool of blood. Remind me never to get on the wrong side of Mona. He was not dead though that seemed to be more by luck than judgement. During the half-hour wait for the ambulance he had time for a full confession, duly recorded on Micah's phone. He knew the data was hidden somewhere in the house and it was just chance that he started on the CD collection.

"And where were you on Wednesday?"

"I was down the..."

"No you weren't. You were killing Tony Sikes."

"That rat. You know he was a mole for Thompsons I suppose. I was doing the world a favour."

I had to restrain Mona who had retrieved the poker. If he hadn't confessed I had thought of letting her loose with it but that would have been unethical.

The epilogue to the story was that Mona was as good as her words. She paid our expenses when the insurance money came through and there was an extra payment for solving the murder.

"She didn't have to do that," Micah said.

"I know but don't tell her that."

Mayhem

"Mayhem."

Our daughter, Dorothy, arrived at the front door. Her clothes seemed to be dripping with blood and she was in the final stages of exhaustion. She was about to collapse into the hallway when Micah appeared.

"Off with those clothes AT ONCE."

"What? Out here?"

"Nobody's watching and I assume your undergarments are clean."

Dorothy, doing a thirty-year-old's version of a stroppy teenager took off her clothes which Micah whisked into the washing machine. She quickly produced a dressing-gown to cover Dorothy's confusion.

"Mayhem?" we asked in unison when she had settled down in an armchair with a large whisky and Barker was licking her toes affectionately.

"We were in Fairholme Woods, a group of people from work, we were paintballing. Hence the state of my clothes. The game was called 'Mayhem' you see."

"Don't they have changing facilities?"

"I don't know because I ran away."

"Why was that?"

"There was a man with a gun."

"Are you sure..."

"Well, he shot someone, dad. Pretty conclusive I'd say!"

Micah was on the phone to the police at once. In half an hour a detective constable was at our door. That is quite quick for these parts.

"Now, Ms McLairy, I understand that you and a few friends were in Fairholme Woods?"

"Yes."

"And you were, I believe the term is 'paintballing'?"

"Yes."

"And you claim to have seen someone shot?"

"Yes. I 'claim' to have seen someone shot. Have you been to the woods? Have you found the body?"

"Now all in good time, Miss. Who was it you saw shot?"

"A nurse from Paediatrics I think."

"You think, miss?"

"To be precise I think he was from Paediatrics. I am absolutely certain he was a nurse."

"I see, miss."

I could see that the 'miss' was beginning to irritate her.

"And could you give the name of this Paediatric nurse, Miss?"

"Certainly, Mike Fuller."

"Ah, well you see, Miss, everybody who was present at this so-called 'paintballing' event has been accounted for except yourself. There was no Mike Fuller present. I think you made a bit of a mistake, dear."

If 'miss' got Dorothy's goat out, "dear" got it out and gave it a good kicking into the bargain.

"So you see, we can take no further action at this time. I will thank you not to waste police time in this way again, dear, or you could be up to your pretty little neck in trouble. Do I make myself clear?"

Dorothy just collapsed into the chair and said no more. This may have been for the best, assaulting an irritating detective constable is a very serious offence.

Detective Constable Harcourt went about his duties.

"Can you describe the murderer?" Micah thought it was a good idea to take up the considerable slack left by the DC.

"He was wearing a green hoodie and I could not see his face. He was of average height but he seemed to be quite athletic. I am judging by the way he ran from the woods after felling the unfortunate Mike Fuller. He killed him with one shot which means he was a good marksman and a very self-confident one. He made no attempt to check that Mike was actually dead."

"And you?"

"I followed the advice you always gave me: "run like hell." It saved my life. I assume the trees made it impossible for him to get a clear shot. He must have seen me unless he was too busy haring away himself. I did not stop to check if Mike Fuller was dead. You always taught me that was a sure-fire way to get myself shot."

I nodded. This was no more than the truth. It was a dictum I picked up in my brief time in the armed services before I was invalided out after an unfortunate disagreement with a nightclub bouncer left me with a bad back.

"Was there anyone else who might have witnessed the murder that never was?"

"Mum, dad, you do believe me don't you? I mean you are the best detective team in Durrington after all."

"Flattery will get you everywhere, young lady. How about a top-up for that whisky?" I suggested.

"Well really I could do with some nosh if that isn't too much trouble."

It is never too much trouble. I love cooking and I soon rustled up an emergency arrabiata with extra chilli which Dorothy wolfed down in short order. We then went on to make some inroads into the single malt and eventually Dorothy got around to answering Micah's question.

"Now I've had time to think about it, I think there were only two paintballers in sight at the time of the 'so-called' murder."

"Well let's just call it a murder for now." I said.

Dorothy smiled. "They were Losie and Bosie, two theatre nurses. They were canoodling behind a sycamore."

"Are you sure?"

"Well it might have been a plain tree. You never taught me any nature study did you?"

"Do they have proper names?"

"Now, mum, you don't have to sound like an old maiden aunt. Their names are Louise Harper and Boris Harper. He hates the name Boris because of that Boris Johnson idiot. Louise was always called Losie so he became Bosie. I bet you had nicknames when you were young."

"Yes, your father's was four-eyes,"

"And yours was..."

"Shut up."

I shut up. Dorothy indicated she wanted to return home for a sleep as she had an early shift the next day.

We made arrangements to take Barker round to visit the Harpers. Apparently they like dogs.

Losie and Bosie, as I suppose I must call them, lived in a flat overlooking the railway station. They were forbidden to have any pets so they were delighted with Barker and fed him up with more treats than were probably good for him. He raised no objection.

"Did you enjoy the paintballing?"

"It was good fun to see everybody out of a work setting I suppose," said Bosie, "and there were plenty of drinks. I took a bottle of Jagermeister and we managed to get through it nicely."

"Did you see Mike Fuller?"

We both saw the glance which passed between them. It was Losie who answered us.

"What makes you think he was there?"

"Our daughter, Dorothy McLairy was there and she saw him. We were wondering if you had seen him as well."

"We didn't see him at all," said Losie and Bosie just nodded.

"Did you see anybody else? Somebody who wasn't one of the group? A man in a green hoodie?"

"This was Fairholme Woods not Sherwood Forest. We didn't see Robin Hood or anyone in Lincoln Green."

"Well it has been nice talking to you. Has DC Harcourt been in touch?"

"Yes."

"No."

They spoke almost simultaneously.

"No of course not, my mistake," said Losie.

As we were taking Barker back for his tea, Micah was both angry and elated.

"They were lying their bloody heads off," she exploded.

"But they gave the game away, and it was your question that tripped them up."

"So what do we know?"

"They have seen D C Harcourt."

I nodded.

"And from that fact it seems likely that their other lies are connected with that meeting."

"They claimed, as he did, that Mike Fuller wasn't there. If he really wasn't there…"

"Then there was no murder and Dorothy imagined the whole thing."

"Neither of us believes that. They were so certain that they didn't see him and they didn't see the man in the hoodie. There was no hesitation. There would be in normal circumstances. Normally people would ask each other for confirmation. That made me suspicious. The weedy joke about Robin Hood clinched the matter for me. That had to be a lie."

"So all we have to do is prove it?"

"After tea we can take Barker for a nice walk in Fairholme Woods. If we can't sniff anything out, perhaps he can."

We followed Dorothy's directions to the scene of the crime. There had been some rain and the path was turning rapidly to mud. Darkness was falling.

Near where Mike met his fate, the ground was littered with broken twigs. A poor attempt had been made to cover the tyre tracks but it was obvious that something akin to a Landrover had crashed through the trees. It had headed straight from the roadway and reversed. Alternatively, it reversed in and went out forwards.

No doubt Sherlock could have detected the direction of the vehicle or the presence of traces of blood or signs of a body being dragged but for us, the crime scene had been hopelessly compromised. Everything was muddy, wet and twiggy. Even Barker's ability to sniff things out were of no use to us.

"It might have been deliberate," Micah said.

"It might as well have been," I answered.

We photographed the scene as best we could and went home to mull some wine and mull over the circumstances.

It wasn't long before Micah pulled out her laptop and started using her dark arts to hack into the local police computer. She kept up a running commentary.

"There hasn't been an incident at Fairholme Woods since last year when there was a complaint about a scout master and he was arrested for flashing some passing ladies in the woods. There is no record of any other incident nor of Dorothy 'wasting police time' which is interesting."

"They have nothing about Mike Fuller or about Losie and Bosie. No records. Not so much as a parking ticket. Ah, that's interesting."

She liked to keep me waiting to find out what was 'interesting'. Eventually, she broke her silence.

"There is no record of any Detective Constable Harcourt, past, present or future. There is no Hardcourt or anything similar. I did a fuzzy logic search."

"I saw his warrant card."

"A clever forgery. Actually not so clever now practically everyone has a scanner and printer." Micah dismissed that detail.

"So could he be from another station?"

"It is unlikely but I will check."

She concentrated on the laptop for an hour and a half. I settled down and poured us out drinks. Hers remained untouched until she had completed her researches with fuzzy felt or whatever.

Before she told me anything she took a large drink.

"No there is a DC Hardcourt in Manchester and a Harcourt in Bromsgrove but there is none in the whole of Sussex. Our man was a fake and a very audacious one."

"Just think. He turned up here, flashed his fake ID and accused Dorothy of wasting police time. He must have realised we would be onto him as soon as Mike Fuller failed to turn up at work. The police would be notified in due course but we could hurry things along a little."

"Surely he was impersonating a police officer and that is a serious criminal matter," I said.

"Yes it is but I think he was guilty of a far more serious offence than that."

A phone-call from Dorothy confirmed that Mike had indeed failed to turn up for work so the police had been informed. A check on his flat confirmed that he had just vanished.

A check on the stock of morphine at the hospital, to which Mike had access, revealed that a lot of it had gone missing over a period of a few months and the hospital was facing a shortage. They couldn't afford to buy any more but they couldn't afford not to either.

"That should, at last, shake the police out of their complacency," she concluded.

While I put the sausages in the oven for tea and got to work on the onion gravy, Micah kept up a running commentary on her researches.

"You know the hospital has a water-tight firewall."

"Can you have a water-tight firewall?"

"Shut up, Craig. They have very good security on their computer system. I know because I helped Dorothy install it."

"And in the process of installing it?"

"I had to include a trapdoor."

"So you could jump out like the demon king?"

"So I could test the system," she explained patiently, "I sometimes wonder if you are as daft as you seem. I set up the system so that Dorothy or I could get into it. That is what I am doing now."

"Now this is interesting. It seems Mike was facing a disciplinary. Someone had leaked to senior management his comments on a private network called "#Staffrage" where people were free to let off steam about their bosses. It seems Mike had a bust-up with his immediate boss, Cathy Grant. It started out like an angry outburst about her authoritarian style but it quickly became some very nasty stuff."

"Cathy Grant was sent some disgusting messages, photoshopped images of her face with a naked body (so she says) in a number of compromising positions. No, you can't look at them. I think I should have a chat with Cathy Grant."

"Dorothy is certain the murderer was a man not a woman."

"I am glad your brain has come back from its holiday. Yes, I remember that but of course, she might have had an accomplice. I just want to know what her attitude to Mike was and whether she regarded this as typical behaviour or out of character for him."

I took Barker out for a pleasant, if rather cold, walk through some of the twittens of Durrington and then he and I waited at home for Micah to return. As usual, she had recorded the conversation on her smartphone. (I believe that is slightly illegal so keep it to yourself). She fast forwarded to the bit she thought relevant.

"Those compromising photographs of you aren't photoshopped are they?" It was Micah's voice and it was really more of a statement than a question.

There was a long pause.

Cathy mumbled.

"Sorry Miss Grant I didn't hear that.

"How did you know?"

"I have been a detective for a long time," was all Micah said. She confided to me that it was in fact just an educated guess.

"Look, you don't have to tell senior management about this do you?"

"I don't have to tell anybody at the hospital about it," said Micah.

There was another pause. Then Cathy Grant spoke in a breathless rush.

"I met Chas at a club. He was very charming at first and I enjoyed his company but there was a side to him that I never knew, do you know that song?"

"So you met charming Chas at a club?" Micah prompted.

"He kept buying me drinks. He must have slipped flunitrazepam into one of the drinks. I was drinking shots. It's also called Rohypnol, you know."

"Doesn't that turn drinks blue?"

"That's why I used its generic name. The generic version does not contain any dye."

"And that is when the pictures were taken?"

"I imagine so. I broke off with charming Chas when the son of a bitch tried to blackmail me."

"Do you think Mike had anything to do with sending you those pictures?"

"I just don't know."

"Can you describe Chas?"

"I can do better than that. I took a photo of him in the club. I can email it to you. Are you going to get him arrested?"

"That is the plan. When his attempt to blackmail you failed, we think that he may have tried to blackmail Mike over his unprofessional remarks on #Staffrage. And we have reason to believe that Mike was murdered."

"There is no body though."

"No there isn't."

"So you will never get a murder conviction surely."

"Unless we find the body, of course."

Micah then showed me the picture of Chas. She didn't make any comment. Chas was shown with a friend. I recognised Detective Constable Harcourt at once.

"Just one more thing, " Micah said in a passable imitation of Peter Falk in the role of Columbo, "when this charmer was trying to blackmail you, what exactly was he trying to get from you?"

"What do you mean?"

"I mean was it cash?"

"Well I never found out, I showed him the door."

"That's not strictly true is it?" asked Micah. (Another lucky guess she confided to me).

Cathy's nervous hesitation was apparent from the recording.

Then she sighed.

"Well he was after drugs, diamorphine to be precise. But on my mother's life, the swine never got any of it from me."

I wondered whether she had consulted her mother before offering her life up.

"A lot of morphine did go missing, though." Micah prompted.

"And that is being investigated. However, I never get involved in the physical storage of drugs at my level in the management structure. Sadly I am responsible for the security of all drugs in my department and our foolproof security failed to work."

"Any idea why?"

"Somebody just invented a better fool, I expect. No, honestly the sophisticated accounting procedures were all observed but somebody, possibly Mike, just used a fake key card to do some old-fashioned pilfering."

And Micah left it at that.

"So Chas and Harcourt were both using blackmail to get morphine from the hospital," I said.

Micah nodded and made a note in her notebook.

Looking up, she said, "What do we conclude from that?"

"They were selling it on, that is an awful lot of morphine for personal use. It would kill you. They were prepared to kill Mike Fuller when he stopped providing them with it. Perhaps they intended to use his killing as a warning to Cathy."

"Except that the stocks of morphine were already dangerously low and Cathy claimed not to have access to them anyway," Micah said.

"So that means?"

" It means that for them to keep their customers satisfied they need to source some new product."

"Pardon?"

"Pinch some more morphine. Just let me make a few phone calls."

Micah slipped a new SIM into her phone.

"Hello, this is Cathy. Yes, it does, doesn't it. (Apparently, her contact had said her voice sounded different on the telephone). Confidentially we have had an issue with morphine going missing from store. Our security measures mean that it shouldn't happen but the fact remains that it did. Can I suggest you check your stocks? If you wouldn't mind I would like you to do a very discreet check and ring me back on this number because I don't want it going through the hospital switchboard. Can you do that for me? Thanks everso. I owe you."

"Hello, this is Cathy. Yes, people have told me that..."

It would be a while before the necessary checks could be made so we settled down to some farfalle arabiata and a rather nice bottle of Cabernet Sauvignon while we were waiting.

Micah put the responses on speaker phone. The first one was not encouraging.

"Listen, whoever you are. I have been on the blower to Cathy, we do Pilates every Tuesday at Splashpoint and she knows nothing about this inquiry of yours. Who the devil are you?"

"I am Emma Blaise from Internal Security. We were running a test on your security systems and it is fair to say that you have passed with flying colours. You will be highly commended in my report."

"I don't believe a word of it. I have never heard of Internal Security."

"We could hardly test security if everybody knew about us. Anyway, thank you for your time." Micah terminated the call.

"Emma Blaise?" I asked innocently.

"Well I always quite liked Modesty Blaise and it just popped into my head. Let's hope the other hospital management people I rang aren't as on the ball as that one."

The next call came almost immediately.

"Oh Cathy, thank God you rang me. Although all the security procedures are in place, some scrote has pilfered our store of diamorphine to the tune of about fifty ampoules. We are up that well-known creek without a paddle in sight. Fortunately, we have a suspect, Tracy Woodward, a new member of staff who showed altogether too much interest in our security arrangements in the past week. I am going to have her in tomorrow morning, the minute she comes on shift."

"Don't do that. Can you hold off for a couple of days? Change the key codes by all means but I would rather not alarm Tracy Woodward at this stage. We have a good chance of catching the, well I hardly like to call them masterminds, but the people who may have forced her into this crime. Can you do that for me?"

"Well for a couple of days but I will make a note of the reasons for the delay to cover my backside in case, well just in case."

"Thanks a lot. I owe you."

Micah took the SIM out of the phone and binned it after bending it in half.

"Craig. I think you need to have a discussion with Tracy Woodward."

Over coffee in the depressing hospital canteen the next day I had a casual chat with Tracy Woodward. It seemed that she had ambitions to become a nurse. It also seemed that she was as nervous as a kitten.

When I produced the photo of the dynamic duo she was as strung out as a cat having a nervous breakdown.

"I take it you recognise these two charmers."

"Only one of them," she pointed to Charming Chas.

"Where did you meet him?"

"In a nightclub. I think he put something in my drink, the bastard."

"Rohypnol, or flunitrazepam to use its Sunday name. He has done this before, miss."

There was a silence.

"Were there photographs?"

She nodded.

"I may as well tell you. You are not the one in trouble. Charming Chas and his chum are the ones who are in it up to their necks. There is just one thing I need you to do…"

The Caroline of Brunswick is a truly remarkable pub in Brighton. Their cottage pie is probably the best in the world and their ever-changing décor includes the work of local artists. The décor changes when customers buy things off the wall. It also boasts a tiny comedy venue where the stand-up can walk from the back of the stage to the front in one stride.

On entering you are confronted with a highly realistic but triple-headed wolf which looks as if it wants a piece of you.

We were downstairs in the bar with an old friend from the police force. We were talking mainly about the cuts which were affecting all public services. At the same time, we were earwigging on the conversation at another table.

"This is positively the last time, I tell you. You can stuff your photographs and spread them all over the Argus for all I care," said Tracy.

Chas essayed a sneer and his confederate followed suit.

"I don't think that would be wise, Tracy. I mean I wouldn't harm a hair of your pretty little head but Ralph here," he gestured to his companion, "Well I can't speak for him. He's a dab hand with the old razor."

The phoney DC Harcourt was being cast in the role of bad cop. Our companion was strangely delighted to hear this conversation. He was thinking how it would sound in court.

In the end, Tracy handed over a dozen ampoules with apparent reluctance. In point of fact, they contained saline solution, that's salt water to you and me.

There was a scuffle as our companion handcuffed the charming Chas and Barker made threatening noises to Ralph. It turned out he was petrified of dogs. An on-the-spot search revealed that he was carrying a gun. Our friend looked as if verily his cup was running over when he thought of the charge sheet. Just carrying a gun would put him inside for five years.

The barman, who didn't have any flesh which was not tattooed, took the incident in his stride. Uniformed officers arrived to take the pair away. We bought another round of drinks and matters settled back to normal. I should say what passes for normal in the Caroline of Brunswick.

"Well, McLairy and McLairy have been very useful today," our friend conceded. "This is just as well because you are usually a pain in the arse. Cheers."

"If I could just be a pain in the arse," Micah said, "you will go over the landrover, won't you? There must be forensic evidence of the body of Mike Fuller in it."

"Anything for you, Micah."

Two days later, Micah was using her dark arts to snoop on the police computer network when she gave an ear-splitting whoop of joy.

"They dug up the back garden of Ralph's house. They found the body of Mike Fuller. It had only been buried two feet deep too. Barker could have dug it up."

She stroked Barker's ears to show she didn't really expect him to dig up corpses.

"So Chas and Dave will go down for a long time?"

"Chas and Ralph but yes, I reckon the rozzers got them bang to rights as the saying goes."

Just in Case

Micah is a truly remarkable detective. The John Selden is a truly remarkable pub and we were lunching there as was our wont. The only problem was that although we were the best detective agency in Durrington we didn't have any actual work on hand and the old pension would only stretch to so many dinners even at the John Selden's prices.

John Selden, I may as well mention, since time weighs heavily on my hands, was one of Worthing's most famous sons. Milton described him as "the chief of learned men reputed in this land". The pub is in the vicinity of a cottage where Selden might have lived.

The strains of the theme from Casualty rang out, it was Micah's phone. A case? No, it was her mother who was a case in her own right but not the sort we handle. However, there was the germ of a hint of a shadow of a case in something she said.

"I went to have my hair done and would you believe it, that Sally, you know, the one I always have to do my hair, well she wasn't there. They were very cagey about why she wasn't there so I just had to grin and bear it. Then I found out, you won't believe this, she's only been and gone and got herself arrested. What do you think about that? I mean you could have knocked me down with a feather. You don't expect that sort of thing to happen to people you know, do you?"

"No," Micah always found it easier to agree with her mother, "What was the girl's surname?"

"Well, it was Spencer, nicely alliterative I thought, Sally Spencer."

"And what was Sally Spencer arrested for?"

"Well, I don't know, Micah. I say you're not going to investigate, are you? I mean wearing your detecting hat with that useless husband of yours."

"My useless husband is right next to me," said Micah, loyally. "And of course we will investigate. We will have to rearrange our caseload to make time for it."

Barker was contemplating the barmaid as a potential source of treats. I know for a fact that nobody can resist those big brown eyes for long. When he had got what he was after he started wagging his tail alarmingly as if he wanted to knock over everybody in the bar.

Kultured Kuts, the hair boutique, was nominally unisex. Micah's mother, no mean detective in her own right, had eventually got the manager to confess that they had precisely zero male clients.

Micah effectively volunteered to visit the salon to find out how much they knew. Their charges almost made all my hair fall out. I could have been their first male customer by proxy.

"Isn't it terrible about Sally Spencer?"

"Why? What happened to her?"

Micah didn't have to answer that one because a colleague was only too pleased to fill in the acolyte who was tending Micah's locks.

"Didn't you hear? It's always the quiet ones isn't it, Mrs M? Who would have thought that Sally who worked alongside me, was all the time one of those terrorists? It gives me cold shivers just to think about it. We could all have been murdered if they hadn't caught up with her."

"Pardon?" the girl dressing Micah's hair so expensively wouldn't have that version of events. "I thought she was just off with the 'flu. You must have got it all wrong. Sally wouldn't harm a hair of anyone's head. Just as well given she was a professional hairdresser."

"You'd better get on with dealing with your client. I'm so sorry, Mrs M, we just can't get the staff these days."

Micah's smartphone then recorded a later conversation with the girl who knew so much.

"Well I got it from Vicky and she got it from Cassie. Sally had been picked up by the fuzz, I mean arrested by the security services, and the chilling thing is she was handed over to the Special Branch because of the terrorist connections in the case. What do you think about that?"

"Cassie?"

"Yes well she should know, her boyfriend, Dick, is in the filth, I mean he's a police officer. Actually, he's a Community Support Officer technically speaking."

"Do you think I could have a word with Cassie?"

"Of course, as soon as she gets back from Ibiza by which I mean if she ever comes back. Cassie left under a bit of a cloud, takings vanishing from the till, that sort of thing."

I speculated that one haircut could finance a month in Ibiza but Micah just gave me a look. Nobody who has been on the receiving end of one of Micah's looks fails to get the point. I started talking about my plans for dinner.

"Surely the police have to release the poor girl within 24 hours if they find her innocent," I said while cutting up the chicken.

"Twenty-eight." said Micah, while slicing the red peppers and onions.

"Why 28 hours? That seems an odd number."

"Twenty-eight has always been an even number, Craig, but it is 28 days not hours. In that time it is assumed anybody would have confessed to anything."

"Surely she must have been in possession of bomb-making equipment or firearms or something."

"Oh try to keep up, Craig. Terrorism can be defined as having an opinion."

"Opinions are illegal?"

"I am sure most of yours are. Now let's put this lot in the oven and have a drink."

I poured out two generous glasses of Bulgarian Cabernet Sauvignon and we sat by the fire with Barker hogging most of it. It was a cosy domestic scene, far removed from the authoritarian state we seemed to be living in.

Later that evening Micah was working on her laptop and she let out the sort of swear word one does not associate with a convent-educated woman. I may not be acquainted with enough convent-educated women to judge.

"You know, the anti-terrorist police have got serious security on their computer system. I can only get information from our local nick and that just says that Sally Spencer, has been detained on terrorist offences (unspecified) and being investigated by Section T which I assume to be the anti-terror squad. Section T has proper encryption and protection."

"Can we expect a knock on the door in the night, then?"

"Don't be ridiculous, Craig. You should know I passed this activity through a number of spoof IP addresses and we are no more likely to be caught than Houdini."

At that moment there was a knock on the door. And it was indeed night-time.

At the door was a man in uniform and a high-visibility jacket. His jacket, I noticed had the word "Police" in large letters and "Community Support Officer" in much smaller letters. The CSOs used to get a lot of stick from the general public and resented the name 'plastic plods' which seemed to stick to them.

"Mr Craig McLairy?"

"Yes, Mr Travis."

"How do you know my name?"

I pointed wordlessly to the name badge "Richard Travis, Community Support Officer". I thought this might be the Dick who was going out with Cassie. I wondered how he liked her enjoying herself in Ibiza while he patrolled the rainy streets of Durrington.

"I wish to speak to," he consulted his notebook, "Mr Micah McLairy."

"Mrs Micah McLairy," Micah corrected him, giving a smile to take the edge off the implied criticism.

"Do come in, Mr Travis," she continued politely.

He stood dripping rainwater onto our carpet. Barker eyed him warily and growled softly.

"Put that animal away! That's a dangerous dog that is. Put it away, I tell you!"

Barker is about as dangerous as a teddy bear but I took him off to the kitchen anyway. He then started whining and scratching at the door because he wanted to get back in front of the fire.

"Mrs McLairy," he continued when he had calmed down, "could you tell me your precise relationship with Sally Spencer?"

"She is my mother's hairdresser."

"You mother being?"

"Mrs Dunbar."

"Address?"

Micah duly gave the address. Her mother still lived in the same house Micah had been brought up in.

"You are aware that Ms Spencer has been detained on terrorist charges?"

"I have never met Sally but I was told today by one of her colleagues that she had been arrested, yes."

"And you are aware that aiding and abetting a terrorist carries a sentence of up to ten years' imprisonment?"

"Asking a single question in a hair boutique is hardly aiding and abetting."

"I would advise you, both of you, not to be argumentative. You can consider this a warning. Assisting a terrorist is an act of terrorism and the law will come down on the pair of you like a ton of bricks. There is no appeal and no evidence is required. You will not interfere in this case. Do I make myself clear?"

"Yes, Mr Travis," Micah said. I agreed.

"Would you like a cup of tea?"

Dick Travis looked at Micah as if she had offered him a giraffe.

"Just be warned. Keep your nose out of Sally Spencer's case. Or else."

He essayed a threatening look and let himself out.

We let Barker back in and tried to resume our cosy evening. It wasn't easy because Barker was in a mood and started prowling around the living room as if he thought Dick was hiding somewhere.

I took him out for a walk in the rain. He was as keen on walks in the rain as I am, which is not much. However, needs must.

When I got back, I could see straight away that Micah was in a fury.

"Mum has just been on the phone. That lout Travis has been round and given her the same warning he gave to us. 'You wouldn't want to see your daughter locked up in prison now would you, Mrs Dunbar?' and all that jazz. I'd like to ram his walkie-talkie up his backside!"

"Micah, do you think he was acting on orders or acting alone?"

"Well they wouldn't send a plastic plod round to do a grown man's work, would they? So I think we can go with 'acting alone'. I think," and here she paused to think, "I think we should find out where Travis lives. It is just possible he will lead us to Cassie. I don't believe she is still in Ibiza. The two of them would have gone together if they are really an item."

"We can't get to Sally. Not even a lawyer can do that. No lawyer wants to go down for aiding and abetting a terrorist and providing a defence would come under that heading. So we'll just have to see what we can do," she paused for a minute and gave that smile which always meant she had come up with a cunning plan.

We got into Micah's old car with its "Stop Rhino Poaching" sticker in the back window. I must say it is pretty effective. There has been no reported rhino poaching in Durrington since she got it.

We parked two streets away from Travis's address. Micah had used her dark arts on the laptop to find where he lived. She goggled him or something apparently. We then made use of the fascinating network of twittens with which Durrington is richly provided to get closer to what she now called "our target". On the way, she continued on the issue of whether our Dick was really an anti-terrorist officer or just too big for his boots.

"He was wearing a high-visibility jacket. I don't know about you but I always think of spies as being more low-visibility myself. His job is probably with traffic but he likes to think he's James Bond and in his fantasies he is. He is a man who likes to throw his weight around, particularly with old women like mum who will be impressed with his machismo."

"Guys who think they're macho," I ventured.

"Usually aren't mucho," Micah completed the quotation from Zsa Zsa Gabor.

"Anyway, I really must return his notebook."

"Micah," I said.

"What?" Micah answered innocently, "he left it behind by accident. I didn't steal it. Well, not as such."

"Anything interesting in it?"

"That young man has dreadful handwriting and spelling. There were several pages of car numbers so my suggestion of traffic control being his forte wasn't a complete shot in the dark. Unless he is the car equivalent of a trainspotter. Then there was an interesting page quoting the anti-terrorist legislation with reference to photographing police officers and having material which would help terrorists. He lists 'Fahrenheit 911" although he misspells Fahrenheit."

We arrived at the house, it was a pebbledashed semi. The garden could do with a bit of work, or a flood to clean it up a bit. We knocked on the door. There was no reply for a while but then lights started going on and eventually a bleary-eyed Dick opened the door. He was half asleep and clearly outraged at being on the receiving end of a 'knock on the door in the night'. He could give it out but not take it.

He snatched the book and barely thanked Micah before slamming the door on us. A voice from within asked querulously who was at the door and was told to shut up.

As we walked back to the car, Micah was quietly pleased with herself. She hummed on the way home.

"I can tell you one thing," she seemed to be addressing Barker, "there was a distinct aroma of Eau de Parfum de Paris and I can't imagine that lumpy lout spraying it on himself.

"My mother," she said to me as she picked up her mobile phone, "has a very fine nose."

After a long conversation which strayed into issues of hair boutiques and perfume, she looked at me and said, "Devious little bastard."

I must have looked affronted because she then felt constrained to add, "Not you, you clot. Dick Travis."

"First off he hacked into the police computer. Now don't look at me like that. I haven't gone over to the dark side like Tricky Dicky. He put a record about Sally Spencer being arrested on their system. You wouldn't find it unless you were looking for it and none of them had any reason to look for it.

"We know Cassie is a pilfering little madam so it is just possible that she filched Sally's perfume. My mother is absolutely certain that Cassie favours Coco Chanel so I don't see her taking Eau de Parfum de Paris from Sally.

"Mark my words, Craig. Sally is being held in that house against her will. 'Step outside and you will be locked up as a terrorist.' that kind of threat would keep her under cover, wouldn't it. At least to start with. After that, Dick would have to use other methods of restraint. You have to break into that house."

I looked at her. She looked at me. "I mean we have to break into that house."

Micah is a first-rate detective, as I have said before. I am a first-rate lurker. Micah stayed in the warm car. I lurked in the cold in a conveniently-positioned twitten to observe. First, our Dick went out in his high-visibility jacket to pursue his traffic career. I sincerely hoped it would be the last time he did that. Cassie kissed him goodbye.

Cassie left for work fifteen minutes later.

I sent a text to Micah and after five minutes I approached the front door. I knocked on the door and rang the bell but answer came there none.

Eventually, the door was answered by Micah. She is a dab hand at housebreaking when the occasion demands it. We searched the downstairs first. Then we started on the upstairs.

"Who are you?"

We introduced ourselves to the woman who was locked into a small upstairs room. She looked as if she hadn't been fed for days. The blinds were pulled down.

"And can I take it you are Sally Spencer?"

"What if I am?"

"We think Dick and Cassie are holding you here against your will as a domestic slave."

"They were friends of mine."

I looked pointedly at the iron chain she had around her ankle.

"I said 'were'," she explained.

"Then they threatened you with a whole load of hooey about the Prevention of Terrorism Act." said Micah.

She nodded.

"I am here to tell you that you cannot go to prison for photographing a Community Support Officer – the law is quite explicit on this. As for Fahrenheit 9/11, it was shown at the Connaught Cinema and nobody has locked them up."

"However the people who will go to prison are Cassie and Dick," I added.

And they did.

When we were home after taking Sally to the police station to make a statement, Micah pointed out that we actually hadn't been paid for this work.

"It was good practice for when we do get a proper case."

"Just in case, " said Micah with a smile.

The Mystery of Swan House

Swan House was in the posher part of Salvington, properly known as High Salvington. It was the residence of Colonel Roger "Rogue" Withers, formerly of the Royal Artillery. After an undistinguished military career during which he was repeatedly not mentioned in dispatches, he was appointed to the job of inspector in the Sharpdale constabulary where he continued to fail to impress.

For the colonel to receive an invitation to join a football team, the Sharpdale Old Boys, must have been a bit of a surprise since he had scarcely stirred from his wheelchair in five years since his retirement. That does not explain why it made him take his old service revolver and blow his brains out.

The colonel's suicide was the talk of the John Selden. There was a lot of sympathy expressed for his housekeeper, Maria Doats. She had followed the fine tradition established in the TV series of Poirot and Marple by dropping a breakfast tray and distributing its contents all over the colonel's study when she discovered the macabre scene.

According to the Worthing Herald, the police were not treating his death as suspicious. Not only did the colonel not have any arguments with his neighbours, most of them didn't know he existed. He had no living relatives and his money was left to a Sharpdale cat's home.

"You don't think the moggies did him in then?" Micah asked.

"No I don't but there was no suicide note."

"That is hardly conclusive, twenty percent of suicides don't leave a note."

"Or their relatives destroy it of course."

"No relatives in this case."

"Who was pathologist?"

"Dr Leaf and he is a well-respected one, not like that blundering windbag Winter. I would automatically suspect foul play if he were involved."

"So there is nothing to investigate?"

"Except the motive. Why on earth would the colonel want to shuffle off this mortal coil?"

"Depression, incurable illness."

"It was not incurable, he just refused to have a hip replacement. Maria Doats knew the deceased well, having worked for him for five years, he was an even-tempered man. There is no reason to think he took his own life."

Micah considered this. "We haven't enough to go on. Not yet, Craig. We have other work on hand."

Micah was right. We had an insurance investigation of extreme tediousness and it was taking up a lot of our time so we put the colonel on the back burner, so to speak, for the time being.

That is to say right up until the Mayor of Sharpdale suffered a cardiac arrest. One detail which caught my eye was that apparently this fatal event had been precipitated by an invitation his worship received to join the Sharpdale Old Boys' football team.

Our first move was to interview Swan House housekeeper, Maria Doats. We took Barker because it made a good morning walk for him. Micah tracked her down easily using her laptop.

"Hello, hello. Are you a Labrador, boy?"

Barker declined to answer unless you count licking Maria's hand and wagging his tail with enough force to break a leg.

"He's a German Shepherd, that's an Alsatian," I said

"I know what an Alsatian is, I was just being polite. Now, what can I do for you?"

"Now there has been another death associated with the Sharpdale Old Boys' football team, we were wondering if there was anything you could tell us about Colonel Withers."

"Well, he weren't a proper Colonel for a start. He retired years ago and took up a job with the police."

"Are you sure the football club was connected with his..." I hesitated.

"Suicide. Let's use the proper word for it and have done. But who are you to come round asking questions?"

"The Durrington Detective Agency," said Micah, producing our card.

"Durrington," said Mrs Doats with a tone which implied it was a vastly inferior place to Salvington. "Not the proper police then?"

"The police have closed the case as there are no suspicious circumstances."

"Well come in and have a cup of tea. If you can get to the bottom of this mystery then it will be a weight off my mind. I can't get the picture out of my head of the poor old man slumped in his wheelchair with his head blown off.

"There were bits of uugh, I don't like to think about it, brains I suppose, all up the wall. It was the devil to clean up. That was after the police had finished their investigating of course."

"And you are sure the football team invitation was the reason?"

"The colonel was not what you'd call a reflective man. He never had a moment of melancholy in all the time I knew him. And the strange invitation to join the football club was the only piece of real post he got that month I should think. He got the usual advertising rubbish but I was under strict instructions to recycle them. He never looked at them."

As we were leaving, Mrs Doats seemed to remember something, "Durrington Detectives, Mr McLairy. Ah yes. I think you know my daughter, Mary? She used to be the cook to poor old Doctor Farnsworth. She told me as how you got that ne'er-do-well Gerald put in prison. Good luck to you, to the pair of you. Mind you, the police were satisfied this was suicide."

Micah trawled the newspapers on the subject of Colonel Withers. It turned out that the name "Rogue" was merely a misspelling of his name by the Ministry of War which caused so much amusement in the regiment that he was known by that name for the rest of his military career. That was the only remotely interesting piece of information about him.

The next day was taken up with the tedious insurance job but the day after that found us in Sharpdale. It was a village just an hour's drive away from Durrington. Even Micah's old wreck can get that far without mishap.

Sharpdale is a fine old English village in Sussex built mainly in flint. It seemed that all new building had to follow the flint motif to get planning permission. Councillor Johannes Elderman was responsible for that particular by-law. He was widely regarded as a respectable man, we found out in the Swinging Oak. Local pubs are an excellent source of local gossip but there was no adverse gossip about the man who became mayor only to be struck down in his prime by an unexpected heart attack.

Micah used her dark arts to hack into his medical records. "They really ought to do something about their security" she muttered.

"You mean to make your job harder?"

"I mean provide more of a challenge," she smiled.

"The mayor was on statins like most over-fifties in this country. He was also taking beta blockers so there must have been some concern about his heart. The records don't show a great deal of concern, though. He was offered the usual advice: stop smoking, stop drinking, cut down on the laughing. He was offered it several times so we can assume he never took it."

We arrived at the mayoral residence. The door was opened by a woman straight out of the top drawer. We assumed she was the lady mayoress.

"I have said all I wish to say to the police. You can go about your business."

"We wanted to offer our condolences on your loss."

"Condolences accepted but you can still go about your business. I have had to set the dogs on two reporters so far. Don't make it four."

Barker growled in a way which suggested he thought himself the match of any dog. At his age that was probably not the case so we took him away with us.

"That's a bit of a blow. Where next?" Micah asked.

"Google local sports grounds."

"You have a hunch."

"Yes, I do and stop calling me Quasimodo."

There were three local sports grounds which is quite enough for a small village. One was closed and had been for twenty years though Google hadn't caught up with that yet as the website was still online.

One was still in use and we had a very interesting conversation with the chairperson of the committee. He was a great admirer of Councillor Elderman and thought it was a terrible shame that the village had lost such a down-to-earth character. Micah noted 'down-to-earth" next to "well-respected" in her notebook and we continued on our travels.

Third time lucky, at least it was in this case.

"Ah, you're the detectives who are investigating the death of Johannes Elderman."

News travels fast in a small village.

We asked about the "Old Boys' Club". We had to repeat the question because the chairperson, a Mrs Clark, was a little hard of hearing.

"No. I've never heard of it. There is not much goes on in these parts that I don't get to hear about so it seems as if you're barking up the wrong tree, young man."

Barker chose this point to start licking her toes and she spent a full five minutes fussing him. I could tell he was loving it because his tail nearly broke my shins in its enthusiasm.

This gave her time to think. "Unless of course, you are referring to the old 'Boy's Club' we used to have here years ago. I'll tell you what, young man. If you come back tomorrow I will have a little rifle through my records and see if there is anything about it."

"A terrible shame about Johannes Elderman I thought. He was always quite interested in bringing on the youth of the village. Took an interest in the Boy's Club I imagine but that was years ago and the memory fades. Don't smile, young man. It will come to you too."

This last remark was addressed to Micah so perhaps the eyesight fades as well.

Back in Worthing, I had an interesting call on our telephone. The number is hardly secret, it is on all the business cards of the Durrington Detective Agency. The caller sounded as if he (I was certain it was a 'he') had a heavy cold. It is the sort of effect you get when you hold a hankie over the mouthpiece of an old-fashioned telephone. No doubt there is an app for it on a smartphone.

"Mr Craig McLairy?"

"Yes."

"Are you the one who is investigating the suicide of Colonel Withers?"

"Yes."

"I have some information for you about that. Meet me on the sea front in about an hour from now. Come alone or else."

He detailed whereabouts we were to meet. There is a fair amount of sea front after all.

Not so much as a "please". I decided that 'alone' meant Micah being in the car at a discreet distance and keeping my phone on so she could hear everything. I also decided to take Barker with me. He needed a walk anyway and one is never really alone with a dog, especially one like Barker.

I may or may not be brave but foolhardy, never.

The shades of night were falling fast when Barker and I approached our rendezvous. It was also getting cold. Worthing has a prevailing west wind which can take the flesh off the bones.

It also boasts (or more likely keeps quiet about) the ugliest car park on the South coast. It is rivalled only by the fifteen-story millionaire's tower which overlooks the beach and overshadows half the town. That was where I was to meet this man.

Things did not start well. As the raggedly-dressed young man came towards me, he very quickly produced a very sharp knife and applied it to my throat, not lethally but enough so that I could feel how sharp it was.

"You are going to drop this bloody case. Do you understand me? Drop it or you could be in serious trouble."

This is the kind of thing which upsets me. I don't like it at all. Barker is even less fond of it. Without barking, his bite really is worse than his bark, he sank his teeth into the young man's hand.

Startled, the young hooligan dropped the knife and I retrieved it.

"You realise you can get ten years inside just for carrying this thing, don't you?"

"What are you gonna do? Call the police?" he sneered.

I am quite quick on the uptake for an old timer.

"No, officer, I suggest you arrest yourself."

He blustered for a bit but I had the knife and that usually settles most arguments.

"Just drop the case. Don't say I didn't warn you, sir." The last word was said like an insult. Nothing proved his police credentials more than that turn of phrase. He might as well have flashed his warrant card.

He scarpered pronto. I slipped Barker off the leash and he was soon speeding the young DC on his way. I called him back. The little charmer was no longer a danger.

I did deliver the knife to the police station and gave a fair description of my assailant but I am not naïve enough to expect any results from their inquiries.

"Someone quite high up does not want this suicide investigated," Micah concluded.

"Right now I'd like to investigate a large Cabernet Sauvignon."

"Me too. The John Selden is still open."

While I bought the drinks and a snack which would have fed the eighth army, Micah got to work using her arts on her laptop to hack into the police personnel files and investigate the dark side of the force. Based on my description of the young tearaway on the sea front, she narrowed the identity down to three.

"Is it this one, this one or this one?"

"That one."

"You've identified Detective Constable Jameson. I am putting the mp3 of your conversation with him onto the system. That should make it easier for them to identify your assailant."

"I don't think they are going to do anything."

"Cynic."

"Drink up. Do you agree that someone very senior in the police does not want this story to be told?"

"Yes but why?"

"I think the Colonel's suicide is kosher but there is a story about the old 'Boys' Club' which they would rather conceal. We need to follow it up."

"How?"

"Well, Mrs Clark's records might give us some leads on the former members of the Boys' Club. I can't help feeling it is too much of a coincidence. Withers was stationed in Sharpdene as a police officer. He must have known the mayor."

We had to drag a reluctant Barker from the bar. He received so much fuss and so many treats from the staff that I had considered not feeding him for a week. Barker disputed this idea by standing by his bowl like a sentry until it was filled with food which he wolfed down with no sign of a diminished appetite.

Our trip to Sharpdene was not wasted. Mrs Clark was as good as her word.

"I'm afraid the records don't show the names of any of the boys who took part in the Boys' Club. Or any such records are buried in the mists of time. Can you be buried in a mist? Sorry I digress. They do give the names of the committee."

Micah got out her pad and noted down: Councillor Elderman, Colonel Withers and Councillor Janet Burke JP."

"We know that two of the members are now no longer with us."

"Oh, poor Colonel Withers. He was only trying to do his bit. He was in the police so everything must have been above board." Mrs Clark had a touching faith and it was none of my business to disturb it.

"Councillor Burke?" I prompted.

"Well, Janet Burke is very much alive and kicking. She is kicking the backsides of young hooligans in the magistrate's court. Metaphysically of course."

Micah murmured "metaphorically" beyond the range of Mrs Clark's hearing.

We thanked Mrs Clark. Micah googled the good magistrate and came up with an address not far from the Cricketers' Arms.

"Burke first then lunch?"

She nodded her agreement.

"You're an alsatian aren't you? Who's a good boy then? Who's a good boy?"

It was a while before Councillor Burke would pay any attention to us but then Barker is always a good ice-breaker. She could hardly chuck us out of the house, I reasoned, if she had been fussing Barker.

Naturally she knew all about us and our investigation. She was cagey about her two former fellow committee members but it was clear she thought there was something not quite right.

"The colonel and Johannes were always very interested in the boys. It is not for me to say they were too interested but one does hear such shocking things nowadays.. It must seem to young people that everybody was a paedophile in the old days." She essayed a laugh to make it clear this was not a serious allegation. However the mere fact that she had said it showed how her mind was working.

"Let me show you this."

The councillor's papers were very well-ordered and she was able to lay her hand on the document immediately. She had also kept the envelope.

It was a printed invitation to join the "Old Boys' Football Team".

"I think it might just be one of the lads, well they are hardly lads now, playing a practical joke. The world and his wife has a printer nowadays. I will leave it in your hands in case it helps your investigation. I think, Mr and Mrs, may I call you Craig and Micah?" Taking our assent as granted she continued, "Craig and Micah, you are looking at two deaths which were caused indirectly by this little hoax and I want the perpetrator found. I have also looked out this."

"This" was a list of names and addresses of members of the old "Boys' Club".

"Of course it may be a relative of one of them. It is also likely that some of them have moved. Where I know of a new address through my work as a JP then I have written it in pen on the list. I hope this is all clear?"

"Certainly, Councillor,"

"Janet, please."

"Certainly, Janet. We will let you know the outcome. Thank you very much for your help."

There were a lot of duds on the list. The 'lads' had grown up and moved away. I won't waste your time with them. I had to waste enough time myself. Our first real lead started out unpromisingly. Our list included one Martin Graves.

"Well I haven't seen the bastard in years. And he needn't think he can come whining round here. He walked out the door. He can just keep on walking, as far as I care."

"So you can't tell us where Mr Graves is now?"

"I can tell you exactly where he is now. Down the bloody pub getting out of his brains on snakebite."

"That's cider and lager." She responded to our looks of confusion.

"And the bloody pub?"

"The Dog and Gun. If I had a gun I'd shoot him. I didn't say that. It's just an expression."

They didn't spoil Barker at the Dog and Gun. In fact, despite the name, dogs were banned and guns were discouraged. Micah took her drink out into the garden and Barker, who really preferred the warmth of the bar any day, went reluctantly off with her.

"I tell you what. I tell you what. I tell you what." If I were less experienced I would have expected Martin Graves to be on the verge of telling me something. However, he was slowing down and by the time he got to the third repeat he was snoring peacefully in his corner.

The landlord shrugged as if this was what one had to expect from this customer.

"Does he come in here often?"

"Ah you're McLairy and McLairy aren't you, the private dicks. Old Martin is harmless enough. He cuts up rough sometimes but he is usually too sloshed to see his opponent let alone hit him. I don't think he's your man for the murder of Councillor Elderman. It was murder, though, wasn't it? You should be looking at that stuck-up cow of a wife of his rather than old Martin here."

He paused expectantly.

"Still I am sure you know your own business best. Now, what can I get for you?"

I ordered a house red and 'whatever Martin's having' which did indeed turn out to be Woodpecker and Heineken as he ex had predicted. I settled down next to the recumbent Mr Graves. Once in a while, I jogged the table in hopes his slumbers might be curtailed.

It seemed an age, my watch told me it was fifteen minutes, until he returned to the world of the living. He thanked me for the drink and I attempted to engage him in conversation. This was not as easy as you might think. In the end, I produced the invitation to join the "Old Boys' Football Club" which sent him off into a fit of the giggles. I thought this was progress.

"Have you seen this before?"

"Might've done. Might not."

"It's funny, though, don't you think? I mean you can't imagine the Colonel and the Councillor kicking a football about at their age."

"Councillors, mate, not councillor. That hoity-toity JP who sent me down for being dunking dishorderly got one too. I saw to that."

"So you have seen it before."

"Might have. Might not." He said with a look of cunning and returned to his doze.

While he was dozing, the landlord gave me a wink and carried a galvanised bucket with disinfectant in the bottom over to where Martin was sitting.

"Did you ever see anyone else come in and chat with Martin?" I asked while collecting another house red – it turned out to be an Australian Shiraz. The Shiraz which is exported from New South Wales is very good. I have had cause to regret ordering it in Australia though.

"Well as a rule I would say 'no' but he did have a couple of old mates in here the other night. It must have been a month ago. The Smith brothers, George and John came in. Whatever it was they were discussing they seemed rather grimly amused by the whole affair."

"Can you just show me that flyer you had with you?"

I did. The landlord looked at it.

"Well I couldn't swear to it, you know in court like, but they were discussing something that looked a lot like this."

At this point, Martin awoke and made use of the bucket. There is a reason why most pubs don't serve snakebite. A galvanised bucket is a good precaution. Martin made his way to the toilets and dutifully emptied it while the landlord looked on. He ordered a pint of tap water at the bar.

Martin then started to do the Times crossword. I wouldn't have bet on his chances but he completed it in 14 minutes. Clearing his stomach seemed to have cleared his head. I thought this was a golden opportunity to chat before he started on the snakebite again.

"I didn't know you knew the Smith brothers." I had recognised the names from the list Janet Burke had given me.

"Oh yes, I know them all right. And George could tell you a thing or two about the councillor and the Colonel."

"Such as?"

Martin lowered his voice and looked around the empty bar room in case there were eavesdroppers lurking under the furniture.

"Well John was the younger of them and he always followed George's lead. When George told him to stay away from the old pervs (such was his word) then John obeyed without question. It was a lot later... This is confidential?"

I nodded noncommittally. The pervs, after all, were dead.

"Years later, after a few drinks in here, in fact, George confided in John. The Colonel had taken him out for a little drink after a match. George was well up for that. Old 'call me Johannes' Elderman joined them. They plied him with whisky then they took him out in the Colonel's car and they both interfered with him. Same thing might have happened to me."

"Might have?" I asked.

"Well to be honest I was too drunk to remember much about it but I do remember drinking a lot of whisky. An awful lot in fact."

"They didn't want to kill anybody but the idea of the 'Old Boys' Football Team' was supposed to put the wind up them proper. It seems it did."

"And Janet Burke?"

"Oh 'Janet' is it? She was on the committee and you might say I had a grudge against her. She wasn't an 'old boy' anyway. And she didn't wind up dead. I think that interfering busybody just took it in her stride."

Later the same day I played the recording back to Janet.

"You recorded this on your phone?"

"Yes."

"You didn't get Martin's consent to the recording?"

"No."

I knew what was coming.

"That means it is inadmissible in court. In any case, it is hearsay. If you could get George to make a signed statement..."

"He declined when I spoke to him."

Janet sighed.

"Well, that would appear to be that."

"There is just one thing..." Micah said. She immediately had our full attention.

"Councillor Elderman. He had a heart condition but he wasn't carrying a GTN spray."

"How do you know...no don't tell me. I can check with the police anyway so your unorthodox methods of obtaining information need not be involved."

"You could also check with the chemist. You see he renewed his prescription and collected the new GTN spray a week before his death. I wonder if his wife, Emily, inherits all of his estate?"

"Micah, for crying out loud! You cannot possibly know that."

"Call it an educated guess. Anyway, the ball is in your court now, Janet. The police will not listen to us but they will have to listen to you."

"I will look into it."

Janet was as good as her word. The life-saving GTN spray had been thrown into the rubbish. Remarkably, Emily Elderman's thumbprint was on it.

In the John Selden that night I was jubilant. Micah was quietly pleased but felt she had to add,

"Of course we got no money for that case. Now I've got another insurance job."

She saw my expression when she said this.

"Just think of the bank balance, Craig. Think of the bank balance."

Matrimonial Case

"We don't normally take matrimonial cases," I began.

"We take cases which pay the bills." Micah reminded me.

I had to agree that was true. "...but in your case, Mrs Burrows, we will make an exception. Please continue."

Hannah ("call me Bunny") Burrows was distraught but she mastered her distress to tell us about her matrimonial difficulties.

"We've been married for a good ten years," she turned to Micah, who had started taking notes, "ten years and three months this Tuesday."

"At first everything was fine. We weren't a childless couple in the usual sense. We just didn't want children. We made a joke of that because my maiden name was Rabbits and his name was Burrows."

She essayed a smile but if anything this just made her unhappiness more apparent.

"So when did it start to go wrong?"

"Well, I can't exactly put my finger on it. I thought everything was fine but now I come to think of it, I thought there was something wrong the whole time. I just couldn't tell what it was. He wasn't exactly passionate but then most men aren't are they?"

Micah made a big show of agreeing with her. I was less than pleased about this.

Mrs Burrows continued, "Of late, the last six months perhaps, he has been spending more and more of his time working late. I thought this was nothing odd, he was rising in his profession. He is a draughtsman. It stands to reason that he had deadlines to fulfil and all that nonsense."

"Well one day, about a week ago, I thought I would surprise him by meeting him at work. It turned out that the surprise was on me." She turned on her sad smile again.

"The office, Burrows and Haddock, was closed. There was no sign of him but I can tell you where he was. He was with that…" well I won't repeat her stream of invective but it was not full of terms of endearment "… of a secretary of his. That so-called Trish Gowans. She is no better than she should be and I would bet my last farthing she was at the bottom of all this trouble. I just want you to prove it."

"You are sure you want proof?" Micah asked mildly.

"Yes, I bloody well do."

"I suggest that the next time he is working late, Craig can keep an eye on Miss Gowans and I will come round and have a look at his home computer."

"It's password protected," Mrs Burrows said.

Micah smiled, "I think we have experience in dealing with little problems like that, Mrs Burrows."

Later at the John Selden, we discussed this unusual (for us) case.

"I know we have to pay the bills, darling."

"Enough of the 'darling', Mr McLairy. We are having a serious business discussion here."

I nodded.

"Mrs Burrows does not want proof. She already has this Gowans woman tried, convicted and executed. If our evidence suggests otherwise she will just want another detective agency, and another and another until she gets the answer she wants."

"So you think she just wants the dirt on Patricia Gowans."

"You think the same, don't you?"

"You read minds as well as computers now?"

"Well I can read yours. It's not exactly a three volume novel, is it **darling?** Now buy me a drink, a girl could die of thirst in here."

I got a bottle of Cab Sav. It's cheaper that way than buying it by the glass.

"What do you expect to find on his laptop?" I asked.

"Would he keep anything incriminating there?"

"He would if he thought Bunny wouldn't be able to hack it."

"Lucky Bunny has friends then."

I watched Mrs Gowans' husband decamp. From what he said on the doorstep he was off to the Hare and Hounds. While waiting outside their house it started to rain. A few spots fell to start with of course, to lull me into a false sense of security. They were followed by a downpour.

There was no sign of the erring Frank though. I went home to report my disappointment. The expression on Micah's face told me she had fared rather better.

"I went through the emails but there was nothing of any interest there so I started to look around the old files. There was a video. In fact there were three. My first thought was, why would anybody bother to save porn videos when the internet is full of them? This made me look closer. I have no intention of showing them to you. You get frisky enough anyway. However I took a few stills."

She showed them to me on her phone.

"Isn't that?"

"Yes it is. A younger incarnation of Mrs Burrows."

"Isn't that sweet? He kept some old videos of the good times."

"Now look at the other person in the picture."

I had no idea who it was but it didn't match the picture of Frank Burrows, even if we took account of the passage of time.

"I had to ask 'call me Bunny' of course, she said that it was George. She only knew his first name but she did give me his address She protested that this was all years ago (that much is obvious) and of course it was shot some years before she even met Frank."

"Did she have any idea why they were on his laptop?"

"She seemed genuinely surprised. She said she hadn't been in touch with George for years. Her best guess was that George had found out their address and then sent the videos to Frank out of pure devilment. It was his taste for pure devilment which caused her to break up with George in the first place."

"He never tried to blackmail her?"

"She thought he was capable of it, more than capable. She was adamant that he hadn't tried to do so and, in her words, 'it was all so long ago.'"

"Do you think it might be relevant? Frank thinking, 'what's sauce for the goose is sauce for the gander?'"

"God alone knows where you dredge up these expressions from but I will put that in my notebook in plain English if it's all the same to you."

I smiled and we settled down to a cup of tea. It was one of our rare alcohol-free days.

We were unable to contact George. Micah read the local obituaries and she has a phenomenal memory. George (his last name was Davidson) departed this vale of tears last year. Short of a séance we couldn't hope for any information from him.

His only living relative was a brother in Cardiff who had placed the obituary notice. Of course, the brother might have inherited the gene for devilment along with George so I had a fruitless trip to Cardiff.

"What sort of a chap was your late brother?"

Silence.

"Do you know of any friends he had in Worthing?"

A silence like the other one but longer.

"We have found some videos involving your late brother. Do you know anything about it?"

"Do you have any more questions, Mr McLairy or shall I kick you downstairs now?"

This was said in such a charming tone that I didn't quite realise what Mr Davidson was saying immediately.

I got in one last question on the way out.

"When did you last see your brother?"

"When I was six years' old. Now on your way, Mr McLairy. And don't fall down the stairs, will you?"

When I got home, Micah was looking at a handwritten list of dates. These were the dates on which Frank had been 'working late at the office' possibly with his secretary. However, Micah had an opinion on that.

"I have looked at the timesheets. They are all kept on the computer system at Burrows and Haddock and frankly, I think a ten-year-old could hack their security blindfold. Interestingly Burrows has never claimed overtime because he is a senior partner. That is not particularly surprising. What is surprising is that Ms Patricia Gowans has claimed overtime but the dates do not tally. Sometimes it seems Frank really does work late at the office. Sometimes Ms Gowans has to work late when he is elsewhere but there is no correlation between the dates."

"That could just be the pair of them being sneaky."

Micah looked crestfallen for a moment but then said decisively, "I don't think so."

And that was that.

I have mentioned a certain lack of interest in matrimonial cases already so you can imagine that I perked up considerably while we were listening to the local news in The Black Cat while tucking in to one of their first class breakfasts the following morning.

I caught the tail end of a report, "...the body has been identified as that of prominent local draughtsman, Frank Burrows. We have this comment from his wife, Bunny."

"Mrs Burrows, how do you feel about your husband being carved up with a knife."

"Well of course, I'm over the moon. How the devil do you think I feel you young tyke? Have you lost anyone you love? No? Cat got your tongue. You were so full of yourself a minute ago. Now no more stupid questions. Go away and grow up."

"Mrs Burrows there, the distraught widow."

Micah had her phone out and was trawling the news channels for fully five minutes.

"The body was found on a piece of wasteland in Goring. 'Carved up with a knife' is a fair description. It has also been called 'a frenzied attack'. The knife was left at the scene but there were no usable fingerprints on it. The police are appealing for witnesses," she summarised.

"You mean, 'Did you see someone chopped up with a knife and not mention it to anyone?'" I wondered.

"Yes," said Micah patiently, "or, 'Did you see anybody in this area last night acting suspiciously?' Wandering around late at night is reasonably suspicious behaviour."

"They can't arrest you for it."

"That is not helpful, Craig. Now, are you going to eat that sausage or just leave it on your plate tempting me?"

I handed over the tempting sausage.

"Well, I am having a latte. Then we are going for a walk."

"In this drizzle?"

"You do want to see the scene of the crime."

It wasn't a question.

The scene of the crime was still festooned with police tape blowing in the wind like the debris from a rather sad celebration. There was no police guard and we assumed all the forensic evidence had been removed. That didn't stop us having a good look.

It was an area of rough ground. One or two lads were loitering about and I struck up a conversation with them.

"When are you going to let us come here and play football again?"

They assumed I was the hated fuzz.

"It will be as soon as possible. The inquiries have to be completed. Did any of you see anything?"

"The bloody murder was in the middle of the night. And don't look at me like that. I weren't swearing. It were a bloody murder!"

I agreed. I wasn't sure that none of the lads was around late at night but they all swore they were tucked up in bed by 10.

I must have raised my eyebrows because one lad, a youngster called Harry whose height and impressive crop of acne suggested he was the oldest present, went on to add.

"We weren't asleep obviously. I was still texting until gone midnight."

"Who were you texting?"

"Just mates." He said defensively.

The others volunteered that they had been texting and one let drop the name of Sharon. This sent a wave of sniggers through the group.

"I bet Sharon was up and about in the early hours," said one.

There were more sniggers.

"Not murdering strange blokes, though," Harry said gallantly.

I had to ask for Sharon's number and although they called me a dirty old man, they did volunteer the number. I decided to give the job of talking to Sharon to Micah.

What Sharon had seen was very interesting indeed.

We arranged to see Sharon in The Lamb. She was old enough to drink, she said.

"So, Sharon, have you been exchanging naughty texts with minors?"

"You what? I don't know no miners. Ain't no mines in these parts," Sharon's smile showed she knew perfectly well what Micah meant.

"Harry, John and Luke?"

"Well they're a bit young to be working down pit, aren't they? And I only get texts from Harry and he's sixteen."

"Sixteen?"

"Well, sixteen next birthday. Look, what is all this palaver about? My texts to my mates are nobody's business but my own ain't they?"

"Well we'll leave that aside then, shall we? Harry told us you saw something on the night of the murder."

"This is about the murder, is it? I've already told your lot everything I know and it really isn't much."

I offered to buy the next round but Sharon would have none of it.

"I've got a job of my own. I can pay my way."

"Where do you work?"

"Full of questions aren't you? Typical of the filth."

Micah adopted a "negotiating silence". In the end, people usually speak just to break that silence. They don't always tell the truth of course. When somebody is lying, Micah will always talk about how interesting the fact they have come up with is.

"I work at the newsagents if you must know. You can check any day of the week."

"How do you know Harry?"

"We went to the same school."

"That's interesting. He would have been two or three years younger than you. It is unusual for people in one year to even talk to those in a different year."

"Well, that's where you're wrong. We have a house system. We were in the same house and I had to mentor the younger members. That included Harry and we became mates. Of a sort."

Micah produced a photo of Frank Burrows. Sharon couldn't suppress a smile of amusement.

"Did you see this man?"

"I wouldn't forget a funny face like that. He was going to the waste land. That's where the body was found isn't it?"

Micah nodded.

"Well, I saw he was going that way but I weren't going there myself. I know what people go there for after dark. I will give you a clue, it isn't football."

"Well you couldn't see the football in the dark could you?" Micah said.

Sharon laughed out loud that that. "You're funny," she concluded.

"Was he alone?"

"He was meeting somebody there."

"How do you know?"

"I just know. He wouldn't go there to be on his own would he? And whoever it was done him in. I must have been the last soul to see him alive. Think of that."

"Apart from the killer of course."

"Of course. Now, how about that drink?"

I would not call myself lucky. I have never won on the premium bonds, I buy raffle tickets without expecting to win anything. I like to think my marriage to Micah was more of a stroke of genius than of luck.

The fact we were passing a shop doorway later that night was a lifetime's worth of luck. I pushed Micah so hard into the shop doorway that we ended up in the shop. She didn't have time to ask what the devil I was playing at because I darted outside to get the number of the car which had mounted the pavement in a creditable attempt to bump us off.

"Any luck?"

"There was mud all over the number plate and the back of the car and they went round the corner so fast I had hope the car would roll over."

"Make of car?"

"It was a Ford Fiesta."

"We'd best discuss this at home."

The owner of the late-night grocers was wondering aloud what we were doing in his shop. I pacified him by buying some pilchards.

At home, Micah took out her list of suspects.

Hannah Burrows

Patricia Gowans

Michael Gowans

Next to them, she wrote the makes of their cars. Mr and Mrs Gowans each had a Ford Fiesta. Hannah Burrows was cleared on the grounds that she had a VW Golf and that she had hired us to keep an eye on Frank. That would be strange behaviour for a murderer.

"It is the most common car in the South East of course."

"I would still like to see if either of the Gowan vehicles has mud all over the number plate."

We turned into the Gowans' street. One car was in the road and the other was in the garage. The garage had the noisiest door I have ever come across. Luckily the Gowans were heavy sleepers. sleeping the sleep of the just? I don't think so.

Neither car had the rear number plate obscured but it wasn't necessary. I could tell the minute I entered the garage there was a strong smell of white spirit. Mike Gowans had cleaned off whatever paint he used on the back of the car.

Fortunately he had left the car unlocked. Micah opened and closed the door very quietly.

"We need to know more about Mike Gowan." Micah muttered to herself on the way back home.

"Why did you need to open the car door?"

"Well, you remember Goldfinger?" was her apparently irrelevant response.

"Yes. I saw it at the cinema and then on the TV a couple of times."

"Then do you remember that fictional tracking device James Bond used to track Goldfinger's car?"

"I am guessing it is no longer fictional."

"No, My GPS tracker cost me £31.50 on Amazon. It can be hidden under a bumper or better yet under the dashboard if the owner is daft enough to leave the car unlocked."

She showed me the app on her phone which told us that the car was still in the garage. I refrained from speculating about how useful this information was.

In the middle of the night, I was awakened by a voice. It was coming from Micah's laptop. It was the rather drunken voice Mike Gowans. A somnolent Micah murmured something about a voice-activated microphone, turned over and went back to sleep.

In the morning we both listened to the recording over a cup of tea. It seemed that Mike Gowans was having a long rambling conversation with someone. Clearly, it was someone he did not want Mrs Gowans to know about so he was having it in his car. We had to sit through a lot of this meandering, much of it was incoherent but towards the end, there was one thing which leapt out at me.

"Goodnight, Sekonda."

I looked at Micah. We both knew that name.

"Sekonda" was an unusual name for a woman but I suspected that it was not her real name. The first, or second, thing which would strike you about Sekonda was how little she resembled the late Princess Diana. On her website, there were many pictures which purported to show a resemblance. The clothes were right but everything else was wrong.

She was an escort who provided a range of very reasonably priced services for anyone who wanted a right royal experience and presumably had poor eyesight, a good imagination or both.

Sekonda was also someone who knew everyone in Worthing. If there was anyone she didn't know, she knew somebody who knew them. She was top of our list of people to interview.

All of the people we know keep dog treats. Barker will always deploy those deep brown eyes to make sure that he gets his share. Ideally, he would like more than his share. You will be surprised to learn that there are some people who are not pleased to see us. Sekonda was at best ambivalent. However, she was always pleased to see Barker. She started fussing over him the moment we arrived.

This was time well spent. I am surprised the police don't use friendly dogs like Barker to get suspects in a receptive mood. Police dogs always look as though they would like to take a piece out of you. They eye you up as if you were a butcher's shelf.

Our conversation with Sekonda was delayed because she received a phone call. She then proceeded to tell what might be described as an adult bedtime story to an elderly client. Micah put her hands over my ears. I put my hands over hers. Sekonda looked at the pair of us and raised an eyebrow.

However, the thing I did notice was Sekonda's telephone voice. I had never spoken to her over the telephone. She didn't resemble Princess Diana but she could put on the voice like a pro if that is not an unfortunate turn of phrase.

When she had finished we got straight down to business.

"Mark Gower. He wasn't a client of mine but he was an old schoolmate. He called me on the phone last night. I keep late hours. I expect you were tucked up in bed with your cocoa by then."

"I knew about Frank's murder of course. It was on Heat Radio. I always listen to Heat in the mornings. It gets me out of bed, eventually. Mark was as tired as a newt and I couldn't make much sense of him. What I did pick up was what he was not talking about. He did not say a word about Frank. He was in the same class as Mark. He was more than a friend. They were an item once upon a time. Don't look shocked, Craig. It doesn't suit you."

"Frank married Bunny," she couldn't suppress a snigger at the name, "because a rising draughtsman needed a wife to make him respectable to clients. He thought that being a gay bachelor was not an option. It was like Brokeback Mountain without the fishing. I know they stopped seeing each other after the wedding. That lasted about a month.

"You see, Craig, Mark confided in me. And so did Frank. They wanted somebody to talk to and they knew I wouldn't be shocked. They remembered me at school," she said without emphasis, "when my name was George Whyte."

She stopped to make sure Micah had the spelling right in her notebook. It gave us both time to absorb the information.

Sekonda gave Barker a hug and told him not to be a stranger. Micah suggested that Sekonda might keep asking Mark about Frank's murder in case he had any information. Then we were on our way.

"Where to?" I asked.

"The John Selden of course. Then it might be time for another little visit to your young friend, Sharon.

As we were splitting a bottle of red, Micah remarked,

"So we think the relationship between Mike and Frank is a significant factor?"

"And that Bunny is barking up the wrong tree if that isn't a mixed metaphor?" I added.

Micah nodded and made a note in her book.

"I still think it unlikely that Bunny would put us on the case and then bump off her husband. I still don't rule it out." Micah counted the suspects off on her fingers.

"I don't rule out Trish Gowans. The relationship between Mark and Frank might have been a complete shock to her and she reacted like a woman scorned, than which Hell has no equivalent fury allegedly."

"However, we will see what our young friend has to say and keep our ear tuned in to what Mike has to tell Sekonda assuming he uses the same ruse to communicate with her late at night."

Sharon looked at the photographs.

"Oh, I've seen him all right. I have seen both of them though not together. Maybe they were going to the waste ground. They were going in the right direction. They weren't together. If they were going to pick up girls they wouldn't have gone together now would they?" Sharon was giving valuable information for her glass of lager.

Although I endured Micah's frown and offered Sharon money, she wouldn't have that.

"I've watched cop shows on the telly and that would contaminate my evidence." She brought out the phrase in a passable imitation of Jane Tennyson.

We kept Micah's laptop switched on overnight but we had the sound switched off so none of Mike's midnight maunderings interrupted us. We listened to the recordings over tea in bed in the morning. There was nothing. The same was true for some mornings to come.

Patience is a virtue in this job. It was on the eleventh day that we heard Mike again. As ever he was barely coherent but from his answers it seemed that Sekonda was trying to get something from him about the demise of Frank.

"He was my besh mate, besh mate in all the world," Mike repeated several times but then his tone changed.

"But he changed. Him and that Bunny. It was all 'Bunny this. Bunny that.' It was like a wassisname. You know, one of those things. He drove me mad. He drove me to it. He broke up with me for the last time he said. He was gonna be spectacled from now on. You know spectable, respectable you might say. He drove me to it."

"Drove me to what? Well now that would be telling, wouldn't it? Yes well seeing as it's you I will just drop you a hint. Nobody walks out on me. Do you get it? Nobody."

There were another fifteen minutes of maudlin reflections before he finally fell asleep. It seemed he was using Sekonda as a substitute for counting sheep.

"Was that enough?" I wondered.

"Maybe, maybe not." Micah mused, "We cannot use this recording because it was obtained illegally. Sekonda records her calls 'for training purposes' which is quite legitimate. We will have to persuade her to pass them over to the police though."

Sekonda had her own ideas. The phrase 'nobody leaves me" had stuck in her head and we later found out that she had taken her "recording for training purposes" to Trish Gowans who duly walked out of Mike's life after calling him every name under the sun.

The first we knew about it was a frantic call from Sekonda. She played a recording of a call from a very inebriated Mike which he had made on the land line. He used it quite freely now that Trish was not there to hear.

"I bloody know it was you Shekonda. You can't deny it. Trish has gone and left me and it's all your bloody fault. Well, you are going to pay, you bitch. I will do to you just what I did to that bastard Frank. You see if I don't."

We both went to visit Sekonda. I don't possess an old service revolver but Micah has a very handy Taser which she bought on the internet for 50 dollars so she took that along. We waited and we waited. Sekonda offered us one cup of tea after another while she quietly drank the best part of a bottle of Stolichnaya.

Mike never arrived. He had attempted to drive to Sekonda's and had had a close encounter with a lamppost instead. He did not survive the meeting.

A week later we discussed the case over a drink in the John Selden with Sekonda.

"We don't take matrimonial cases as a rule" Micah began.

"But this one turned out to be more interesting than most," Sekonda concluded.

Also by the author

If you enjoyed this, you will also enjoy the five books in the #mirrorofeternity series.

Stories from the Mirror of Eternity

This is the first in the #mirrorofeternity series. It is a collection of short stories.

In the Mirror of Eternity – This is the first #mirrorofeternity story. It is dangerous to meddle in the past and perhaps even to observe it.

Jack London's Suicide Note – a fictitious exploration of the controversy surrounding Jack London's untimely death at the age of 40.

The Library – an encounter between two very different characters in cyberspace. These days libraries have computers and you can meet all sorts of people online.

Der Der, Der Der – the first Virginia Monologue story. Be warned, she might be quite amusing on the page but give her a wide berth in real life!

Guilt App – A story about the life of the rich and the chasm which exists between them and the 'people of the abyss.'

Paradox – Another adventure in cyberspace. The original story even had screenshots from a Commodore 64 but these have been sacrificed as the C64 now seems even more dated than I am.

Here be dragons – a story which explores the possibilities of travel in time and space. The 'dragon' in question may come as a surprise.

After Spartacus – Spartacus could be regarded as the first socialist – he thought the liberation of the oppressed was a job they could not leave to someone else. The Cross did become a symbol of Rome, but not in the way the Romans of the time imagined it would.

The SS Dagger – using the Mirror of Eternity to solve a murder in Nazi Germany produces an unexpected ending.

League of St George – a harmless drinking club celebrating the myth of St George hides something far more sinister.

The Stalker - I read the tabloid headlines most mornings. If the economy is going down the pan, they will have a headline about Big Brother. If the prime minister is at the centre of a scandal, EastEnders will be the big issue of the day. And I wonder exactly what the truth is behind their celebrity stories.

Virginia Monologue – the second Victoria Monologue story sees her talking to a friend who does not seem to be responding.

Doctor, it's about your car - The best way to get through to someone who is too busy to talk to you is to tell the switchboard "It's about his car." You will get through – even if they are "on a trip abroad" or "in a vital meeting" :)

Dramatoes - Childish pronunciation is always endearing. This story grew out of the way my son pronounced "dominoes".

Omar - This story is based on a personal experience when my wife and I were in Tunisia. I can tell you in advance that the ending was somewhat different in our case but that is all I will tell you before you read it.

The Inspector called - A story about a school inspector. You will have guessed by now that I was a teacher once upon a time and they drove me up the wall. Bear with me.

Schadenfreude - The borderland between waking and sleeping is a strange and sometimes frightening place. It is just as well it is 'all in the mind' isn't it?

The Hitch-hiker - "Don't take lifts from strangers" is all very well. But don't forget the hitch-hiker is a stranger too.

Stations of the Cross - I never "really" believed my father was dead. It was only later, much later, that I realised he wasn't dead. Not as long as he was remembered.

The Tower of the Moon - A romantic tryst with a twist.

When I think about you - This story has been rejected by magazines as "too shocking". So either read it and prepare to be shocked or give it a miss!

Salt Wars

Salt Wars is a myth of the foundation of the city-state of Salzburg. Salt Wars is a science fiction book. It contains mild sex and violence. It also contains some humour.

Xavier Hollands is an eccentric technologist. That sounds so much better than "mad scientist". Using his father's theoretical work he has found a way to create a hard astral projection. After testing this out with his girlfriend, Tilly, he is dragged into the Salt Wars by Wolf-Dietrich von Raitenau who wants to secure the future of Salzburg and his own future as its Prince-Archbishop.

They travel back in time to the town which will eventually become Salzburg. Xavier's astral projection is so strong that he comes into conflict with the "best man" of the town whom he defeats at the May Fair. He also develops a relationship with Krystyna, the daughter of his employer in the town and betrothed of the erstwhile best man.

Using Xavier's methods, Tilly intervenes to save Xavier and to thwart Wolf-Dietrich. Magus – a medieval Satanist – tries to use Krystyna to seduce Xavier and thus tie him to the town forever. When this plot fails because of Tilly's intervention there is a battle through time and space.

Wolf-Dietrich is hunted down like a literal wolf. Xavier meets his claustrophobic nightmare on a submarine which is then depth-charged and flooded with water. Tilly meets her fate in a school where she cannot control her class or stop them bullying a young boy called Gabriel. When Tilly realises that Gabriel is trying to push her towards suicide, he is unmasked as Magus.

The trio return to the town to fight the first salt war. Wolf-Dietrich brings about a successful conclusion by playing on the superstitious fears of the attackers.

The book also has diary entries from the characters which give an insight into their thinking.

The book ends with a teaser for the next Xavier Holland's story "The Archbishop's Torturer"..

The Miranda Revolution

Can a mother's love help bring down a vicious dictatorship? The dictator is a strong man but Miranda is a strong woman.

In this book, three characters, Wolf-Dietrich, Tilly and Xavier become involved with the battle to overthrow the Dictatorship. It is an adventure story in which the three of them fight evil in their own very different ways.

The Dictatorship described is generic and could apply to a number of countries. The gangsters control the streets and the Dictatorship controls the gangsters.

The Dictator's consort, Miranda, is drawn into the revolution by realising one of the street-girls is her daughter. A religious movement which has been a safety valve of value to the Dictator is transformed by Miranda's visions through the 'mirror of eternity'

The Miranda Revolution is a book of light and shade. Although there is humour, there is also a serious side to it. Shelly encouraged the poor to seek a better world with the phrase, "Ye are many, they are few." The poor know only too well that the rich have the guns and tanks on their side. The book is a work of fiction but it suggests one way those problems could be overcome. It is a message of hope.

The Miranda Revolution is suitable for young adults. It contains sex and violence but none of it is graphic. Most of the sexual references illustrate the plight of the street-girls in the Dictatorship.

Defending the Sangreal

The fourth book in the #mirrorofeternity series explores such varied scenes as the realm of Arthurian legend and the dark hidden world of Satanism in the UK.

"Joseph of Aramathea brought Christianity to these islands. He did not bring it in a bloody cup!" (Sir Gareth).

A little blunt but to the point. The Mirror of Eternity 4 gives a new take (Xavier's take) on what the sangreal was all about. It may surprise you. It will give Dan Brown a fit!

So if you have ever wondered what the sangreal (or holy grail) really represented; if you have wondered what kind of horses the four riders of the apocalypse rode or whether there really was a top and bottom of the round table, #mirrorofeternity4 will answer your questions. From a certain point of view.

This book will make you want to know more about the knights of the soi-disant 'round table' and about the Mirror of Eternity. It might make you want to avoid Satanism and Satanists like the plague. It will certainly intrigue you.

Space Dog Alfred

Space Dog Alfred is not part of the #mirrorofeternity series and it is aimed at a younger audience. It is the book which has had most success in the difficult business of getting libraries ,which have no money to spare, to buy copies.

The book tells the story of a French Bulldog who ends up going into space with Finbar Cool, a very dodgy street trader and uncle to Tom and Seren, the twins who accompany him. Finn brings his daughter, Abby, along too. Tom is delighted about Abby tagging along, Seren not so much.

On the planet they visit there is a group mind which is shared by Gai - sentient tree-like creatures - the Veck who are humans but have mastered unpowered flight and the people of Ardin who are small but perfectly formed. They worship death.

The group mind is not shared by creatures known as the Gnarl who are warlike and largely live underground.

It is an adventure story in which the powers of all the characters are tested to the maximum. Abby, captured by the slovenly Veck, realises that her selfishness is holding her back. Seren eventually comes to realise that Abby can change for the better. Tom finds out that he really doesn't know everything. Finn realises the futility of war. Alfred's bravery and his powers of perception make him into a hero. Like all French Bulldogs, he has the power to understand what humans (and other creatures) are thinking.

In the end good triumphs over evil. The heroes succeed in averting a war which would have cost thousands of lives. In doing so they also introduce the gnarl to the joy of storytelling. They prove that it is possible to win a battle by surrendering.

Domain of Dreams

In this book, I have returned to the short story format. I have had some success in selling short stories in the United States to *Everyday Fiction* and to *Page and Spine* and in Canada to *Saturday Night Reader*. I even had one published in the Worthing Herald! It has something for everyone – adventure, romance, mystery and humour. I put into my stories the things I like to read myself. I expect all writers do that :)

The Mirror of Eternity is a computer simulation which enables the user to look backwards (and occasionally forwards) in time. It deals with the paradox of time travel. Although science categorically tells you that you cannot travel in time, in your dreams and reveries you can go to any place and any time. I think that Domain of Dreams takes full advantage of the possibilities of the Mirror of Eternity. Opinions differ as to whether it provides access to a parallel universe or its effects are simply an illusion.

The main characters are Wolf-Dietrich von Raitenau, the Prince-Archbishop of Salzburg. Xavier Hollands, the eccentric technologist, his wife Tilly who shares the programming of the Mirror of Eternity and the narrator who has remained a shadowy figure in the previous four books.

I love the scope and freedom which Science Fiction and Fantasy brings. I also like the discipline of the short story. As Mark Twain said in apologising for writing a long letter to a friend, "I didn't have the time to write a short one."

I started writing when I was ten but I have been able to devote the time to it since I retired 50 years later. I have learnt a lot in the last five years both about writing and about the market for books. I have had some success in selling my self-published books to libraries and bookshops but it has been an interesting challenge.

My greatest joy is sharing my ideas with my wife, Angela, who is also my editor.

Note – I intended to call the book "Dreamscape" but there are a surprising number of books with that title.

Printed in Great Britain
by Amazon